THREE BY PEREC

GEORGES PEREC

THREE BY PEREC

WHICH MOPED WITH CHROME-PLATED
HANDLEBARS AT THE BACK OF THE YARD?

THE EXETER TEXT: JEWELS, SECRETS, SEX

A GALLERY PORTRAIT

Translated from the French by Ian Monk

Introductions by David Bellos

A Verba Mundi Book

David R. Godine · Publisher · Boston

This is a *Verba Mundi* Book
published in 2004 by
DAVID R. GODINE, *Publisher*
Post Office Box 450
Jaffrey, New Hampshire 03452
www.godine.com

Which Moped with Chrome-plated Handlebars at the Back of the Yard?
First published in France with the title
Quel petit vélo à guidon chromé au fond de la cour?
by Les Lettres Nouvelles, Paris, 1966
© Editions Denoël, 1966

The Exeter Text: Jewels, Secrets, Sex
First published in France with the title *Les Revenentes*
by Editions Julliard, Paris, 1972
© Editions Julliard, 1972, 1991

A Gallery Portrait
First published in France with the title *Un cabinet d'amateur*
by Editions André Balland, Paris, 1979
© Editions Balland, 1979, 1988

The three works first published in Great Britain in one volume
in 1996 by The Harvill Press, 84 Thornhill Road, London N1 1RD

English translations © The Harvill Press 1996
Introductions © David Bellos 1996

LIBRARY OF CONGRESS CATALOGING-IN-PUBLICATION DATA
Perec, Georges, 1936–1982.
[Short stories. English. Selections]
Three by Perec / Georges Perec ; translated from the French by Ian Monk ;
introductions by David Bellos.
p. cm. (A Verba Mundi Book)
Includes bibliographical references and index.
ISBN 1-56792-254-6 (alk. paper)
I. Title: 3 by Perec. II. Monk, Ian. III. Perec, Georges, 1936–1982. Quel petit vélo
à guidon chromé au fond de la cour? English. IV. Perec, Georges, 1936–1982.
Revenentes. English. V. Perec, Georges, 1936–1982. Cabinet d'amateur. English.
VI. Title. VII. Verba Mundi.
PQ2676.E67A26 20048   43'.914—DC22
2004006347

FIRST PRINTING
Printed in Canada

CONTENTS

PUBLISHER'S NOTE

In January 1982, a few weeks before his death at the age of 46, Georges Perec wrote to the publisher Christian Bourgois to suggest that three of his shorter books – all of them literary amusements, "ludic" novellas written at different stages of his career – should be brought together in one volume. The present set of translations thus fulfils one of Georges Perec's last wishes, as yet unrealized in French.

.

WHICH MOPED WITH CHROME-PLATED
HANDLEBARS AT THE BACK OF THE YARD?

*This tale is dedicated to the memory
of L. G.'s finest feat of arms
(and I'm not kidding you).*

Georges Perec

WHICH MOPED WITH CHROME-PLATED HANDLEBARS AT THE BACK OF THE YARD?

Epic prose tale embellished with
versified ornamentations
taken from the finest authors

by the author of
*How to Do
Your Friends
a Good Turn*
*(this work has been awarded prizes
by numerous Military Academies)*

A VERBA MUNDI BOOK
David R. Godine · *Publisher* · *Boston*

INTRODUCTION

DAVID BELLOS

Georges Perec finished correcting the proofs of *Things*, the first of his novels to be accepted by a publisher, in the early summer of 1965. The book was scheduled to appear in September. In the meantime, Perec remained an unknown twenty-nine-year-old Left Bank intellectual with high ambitions and a caustic, often self-deprecating wit. *Which Moped with Chrome-plated Handlebars at the Back of the Yard?* was written then, not as a sequel to *Things*, but almost as an antidote to taking literary ambition too seriously. *Which Moped...?* is a light-hearted game with the language of literature, with the rules of rhetoric, and the conventions of novel-writing – beginning with the title, just about the most implausible title phrase ever turned. Rules of spelling and grammar are broken in almost every sentence; basic conventions – such as the consistency of characters' names – are turned upside down. Perec exploits to the full the humorous potential of mixing stylistic registers, producing a comical juxtaposition of spoken and written, informal and formal, vulgar and high-flown language that is the diametrical opposite of the controlled and classical writing of *Things*.

However, *Which Moped...?* is not just a high-spirited exercise in literary aggression. It tells the story of an attempt by a group of Parisian intellectuals to save a conscript from being drafted to the war zone in the closing stages of the Algerian conflict, and it is closely based on a real event in which Georges Perec took part. Beneath their fictional names, individual members of Perec's social circle are clearly identifiable. The underlying issue of this literary entertainment is not comical at all, but had been a vitally serious one for the generation of French people who came into adulthood in the course of the unpopular and unwinnable Algerian War: whether or not to implement their principled belief in passive resistance, and to put themselves beyond the law.

It is therefore no coincidence that *Which Moped...?* is dedicated to "Lg", standing for *La Ligne générale* ("The General Line"). It was the name taken (from Eisenstein's celebrated film, also known as *The Old and the New*) by the group which had provided Perec with his first significant "family of friends" as well as his second education. Lg was founded in 1958 with the aim of launching a new journal of literature and art that would revitalize and redirect French culture in the 1960s, and occupy the same high ground that Sartre's *Les Temps modernes* had done in the 1950s. It sought to reinvigorate Marxist approaches to modern culture, whilst remaining outside of the control of the Communist Party, then a dominating influence in French intellectual and cultural life. Perec had been one of the two leading members of Lg for several years, throughout the period of his military service (1958–1960), his time in Sfax, and his early years as a science librarian in Paris. The envisaged periodical was abandoned, but the group continued to meet for discussions until 1964, when it finally petered out. *Which Moped...?* is Perec's ironical, affectionate farewell to the "fine band of chums" called Lg.

Georges Perec became a member of OuLiPo, the "Workshop for Potential Literature", less than two years after writing *Which Moped...?* A comic novella on a serious subject, *Which Moped...?* looks back to the political Perec of the 1950s, and points forward to the unconventional, language-oriented ambitions and skills that the OuLiPo would soon nurture in him, with spectacular results.

THERE WAS ONCE this character called Karamanlis. Or something like that: Karawak? Karawash? Karapet? Well anyway, Karathingy. It was a weird enough name, whatever it was, a name that rang bells, that stuck in your mind.

He might well have been an abstract Armenian from L'Ecole de Paris, a Bulgarian wrestler, a lump of Macedonian fruit jelly, anyway, a character from round thereabouts, a Balkan, a Yoghurtophage, a Slavophile, a Turk.

But right there and then, and for the past fourteen months, he had been a buck private in a transport regiment in Vincennes.

And among his mates figured a bosom pal of ours, Sergeant Henri Pollak himself, exempted from Algeria and overseas service (a sad tale: he'd been an orphan since his tenderest babyhood, an innocent victim, a poor little mite chucked out onto the big city streets at the age of fourteen weeks) and leading a double life: while the sun shone, he would go about his sergeantly duties, bawling out the men on fatigue duties and engraving pierced hearts and abrasive slogans on the latrine doors. But when the half-past of eighteen-hundred hours chimed, he'd straddle his phutting little moped (with chrome-plated handlebars) and, on the wings of a storm, drive back to his native Montparnasse (for he had been born in Montparnasse) where his dearly-beloved was, his digs, us his mates and his darling books, would metaphormose into a dashing youngun, soberly, yet

9

neatly dressed in a green sweater with red stripes, screw-whiff trousers and a pair of the most pump-like pumps imaginable, then come to meet us, his mates, in the cafés where we'd natter on about eats, movies and the meaning of life.

Then, come the morning, our Henri Pollak would slip back into his soldier's uniform, his khaki shirt, his khaki trousers, his khaki kepi, his khaki tie, his khaki jacket, his beige raincoat and his nutbrown shoes, would straddle once more his phutting little moped (with chrome-plated handlebars), would rerun, with his heart in his boots, the journey the other way round, leaving behind him his darling books, us his mates, his digs and his dearly-beloved, even his native Montparnasse (for it was there that he had been bairn) and drive back to Vincennes's Fort Neuf, where a tough day was waiting for him, just like any of the four hundred and seventy-one days which the Mothering Mother of a Sonofabitch of National Service had already put him through, or any of the (but let's not anticipate) three hundred and seventy and nine days that it still would.

Then our Henri Pollak would purse his lips, correct his posture, would pass, chin up, in front of the large three-coloured flag, in front of the guard post, in front of the captain, who he saluted, the lieutenant, who he saluted, the acting adjutant-provisional-assistant-sergeant-major, who he no longer saluted, preferring to change pavements ever since that day when they had had words, and the company men, good old Karascoff, good old Falempain, Van Ostrack (a foul racist) and little Laverrière, warmly nicknamed Ice-Breaker, who would all hail him with assorted bird calls, for he was pretty well-liked was Henri Pollak.

Then a hard day of military travail would begin, with its reports, its calls, its recalls, its mushy peas, its lukewarm beer, its jugs of plonk, its fatigue duties, its thumb-twiddling, its exercises in style, its rusty tincans sent reeling over cropped lawns by skilful boots, its cigarettes, its gaspers, its snout.

And majestic Apollo would so slowly near his Zenith. The hours dragged by as though through an hourglass filled with sandstone (no doubt the reader will deplore this platitudinous image: no matter, let him appreciate its geological pertinence).

And at the long-awaited half-past of eighteen thirty hours, Henri Pollak, our very own mate, would, as long as he wasn't on guard duty, or on fire picket, or confined to barracks, or on a charge, shake Karabinowicz, Falempain, Van Ostrack the foul racist, and little Laverrière (warmly nicknamed Ice-Breaker) by their limp hands, would stuff his night-leave pass, duly stamped by the duty officer, into the left pocket of his khaki jacket, would straddle his phutting little moped (with chrome-plated handlebars), would give the regulation salute to the duty lieutenant, the roster officer, the stand-in adjutant, the locum commander, the sergeant of the week, the corporal of the day and the men on guard, who would applaud him with assorted animal calls, for he was pretty popular was Henri Pollak (salt of the earth, one of the lads, a heart of gold, a real rough diamond) and would wing away like Minerva's fowl at the hour when the lions go down to the waters, would, with the speed of the dreamy-eyed sparrow-hawk, return to his native Montparnasse where first he had seen the light of day and where his dearly-beloved, his digs, us his mates and his darling books were waiting for him, would tear off that despised uniform, would in the twinkling of an eye change into blatant mufti, torso at ease in a cashmere vest, legs snug in a pair of genes, feet firmly shod in weathered, old-world mocassins then come to meet us, his mates, in the café over the road, where we'd speak about Lukasse, Heliphore, Heygal and other oddbodkins tarred with the same brush, for we were all a touch cracked in those days, until the hour was as advanced as our ideas.

Yup, when all is said and done, soldiers led the life of Riley!

But it so fell out that one day, c-rash! all that was to come tumbling down.

It must have been two o'clock, half-past two, maybe even a quarter to three.

And the above-mentioned Karaphone went to see the above-mentioned Henri Pollak (have I said that he was one of our bosom pals?) and, in the words of our celebrated fabulist,

Addressed him more or less as follows:

"A piece of news has come to my astonished ears which left me simultaneously nonplussed, perplexed, pitiable, podagrous and pretty-well putrified: the High, the Most High (blessed be its name) Command is supposed to have decided, nobody is quite sure if it's on some sudden impulse or the fruit of long, mature reflexion, anyway, the High Command is supposed to have decided to give the Captain in Charge of Manning Levels the wearisome task of drawing up a list of those among us who will go off, at the next opportunity, to water with their blood those noble African hills which our glorious history has made into French territories. The name which my family has borne with honour and dignity for five generations and which it passed spotless onto me might, may well even, figure on this list."

And poor old Karaplasm started sobbing like a baby.

"Now, now," said our mate, Sergeant Henri Pollak

gruffly, who would dearly have liked to be somewhere else, in his native Montparnasse for example, where he had been borne, where the love of his life was, his Spartan bedsit, us his mates, and his Oscar bookcase, which he had basely filched from his best friend (that best friend was me).

"Philomachia, fiddlesticks!" Karamagnole went on imperviously. "Cut the belligerency; I don't like war, I don't want to go and fight; I don't want to go to Algeria; I want to stay in Paris where the girl I'm crazy about lives; I want to hug her in my big strong arms."

"Ay? What am I supposed to do about it?" philosophically quipped our friend (Sergeant) Henri Pollak, disturbed by this gush of lyricism.

"My friend, my dear friend, my distinguished colleague, my old china, my good neighbour, my fatted calf," went on this admirable Karalerowicz. "Do not abandon me in my agony, have mercy on me, fly to my succour!"

"Ay? And what am I supposed to do about it?" reiterated Henri Pollak, our mate, sergeant, native of Montparnasse where he was come into the world and where just then were to be found his dearly-intended, his love nest, his little chums (that was us, the little chums) and his bound collection of *Science et Vie*.

"Get in your jeep," the fellow suggested centaurially, "get in your jeep," he repeated, "and run me over. Break my foot so that never more may it be used for murtricidal ends. Then may I, bowed down under pain and affliction, go from military hospital to hospital military. May my fairy-godmother Convalescence touch me with her magic wand. May she grant the longest possible reprieve. And I shall spend it, oh I shall spend it bedded with the girl I am crazy about and then we'll see what we will see. The Algerians'll slip us a Mickey. And peace might even be being signed as we speak."

"What? What?" went friend Henri Pollak, bent double at this extravagant request.

And then explained that – hold your horses – playing the fool without thinking things out first was out of the question, that one had to be circumspect, that he had personal friends (that was us, the personal friends) in the outside world, down civvy-street, in Montparnasse, from where he was a native of, having been born there, and the first thing to do would be to go and ask them what they thought about it all.

Indeed, when the half-past of eighteen-hundred hours chimed, Sergeant Henri Pollak, for whom I'll take this opportunity of assuring to him once again of my undying friendship, straddled his phutting little moped (with chrome-plated handlebars), scattered con-fraternal salutes and nonchalant handshakes all around him, pedalled straight off to his native Montparnasse, which had been witness to his birth and where his only love was, his spick-and-span garret, his lifelong friends, his cultured man's library, extricated himself from that warlike envelope, had a thorough wash and brush-up, picked out a militant get-up, that is to say: linen trousers with matching stitching, an orange cotton crewneck, a collarless teased-veal-skin jacket, a pair of buffalo-hide Jesus boots, sunglasses, the *Observateur Arguments*, an offprint of Arthur Schmildknapp's article about Otto Preminger ("Untersuchungen über das premingerische Weltenbild" *Prolegomena*, 1960, 27: 312–387), came to meet us in the nearby café, and without more ado had he related what was on his mind to us:

That he, Pollak (Henri), a sergeant native of Montparnasse, had a mate called Karaschmerz and that he (Karaschmerz, but also Henri Pollak and everybody else, which is normal at that age) had a girl he was crazy about and that he (still Karaschmerz) displayed a manifest yet nonetheless touching indifference to those differences which confronted, on the one hand, the future of France, and on the other, disreputable bands of trouble-makers and ne'er-do-wells, and that he (Karaschmerz encore) had manifested the desire to stay in France to sleep sweetly between the girl he was crazy about's arms, instead of going off cavorting in the jebels, and that he (i.e. Henri Pollak) had felt as moved as he had been on the day of his first communion and that he had asked what he was supposed to do about it, while saying to himself *in petto* and his heart of hearts that he couldn't do a thing, and that he (Karaschmerz) had suggested that he (Henri Pollak) should run over his foot with a jeep so that once maimed he (Karaschmerz of course) would go to the military hospital and that he (Karaschmerz, evidently) would get a long convalescence and that we (that is to say, everyone in general, and especially Karaschmerz, Henri Pollak, the girls they were crazy about and, just to give him a bit of pleasure, the policeman who directs the traffic at the junction of rue Boris-Vian and boulevard Teilhard-de-Chardin) would have time to sit back and wait and perhaps peace has been signed.

And that he (this time it's definitely friend Henri Pollak, his good self) had said that – hold your horses – it (? quid est this it?) was out of the question to play the fool and that he (the sergeant from Montparnasse, you know, our mate Henri Pollak) was going to speak about all this with his personal friends (that was us, the personal friends) and ask them what they (i.e. we, Henri Pollak's mates) thought about it.

And that there we were, he'd said his say and what did we think?

*   *   *

15

Wheel... the least that can be said is that we didn't think much of it. As a matter of fact, we didn't give a tinker's cuss for his two-bit story about some individual wanting to bail out of Algeria by getting footicapped and then sleeping sweetly between the girl he was crazy about's arms while peace will be being signed. But as, on the one hand, we didn't want to hurt Henri Pollak, our bosom pal's feelings, while on the other, he had so nicely asked us to think and, as everyone knows, thought is life (just look that up in Bergson), two or three of us chewed it over for a bit then went, unconvincingly:

"Ho hum!"

Or else:

"Sure, sure."

Which didn't at all look like it was going to do as far as our Henri Pollak was concerned. Deeply touched by the silent stubbornness which emanated from his intelligent stare, we set about diversifying our appraisals.

A wag sang:

Good old Karaval
'll go to hospital
'n' getta long conval-val...

While others sighed:

"It's all a bit iffy," said the first.

"It's no joke," said the second.

"Sounds bleeding stupid to me," said the third.

"Lawdy, lawdy," said the fourth.

To slum up, our impression was pretty deflavourable.

And then we agreed concertedly and in unison that that person, honourably known under the name of Henri Pollak's driving an automobilized vehicle, which didn't even belong to him, over the foot of some individual we didn't know from Eve or from Adam, even were it be with that person's full and prior consent, was highly undesirable, considering that:

> firstly, he might hurt him, might even hurt him
> very badly;

and that:

> secondly, hobbling, or voluntary pedectomy
> with the sole aim of becoming a non-combat-
> ant must surely be sanctioned by our national
> laws, as much for that person who therein
> willing indulges himself, as for the person or
> persons who had manifestly aided and abetted
> him in his criminal endeavours, or who had,
> though cognisant, not reported the matter to
> the proper authorities.

But really, great Scott! Were we going to abandon a true friend in his hour of need? Would it be said that we, Henri Pollak's mates, had been incapable of assisting that very individual who had, in his despair, been imprudent enough to approach him, Henri Pollak, our dear buddy, his ser-geant, but nevertheless his friend, with an appeal for his aid? Would it be said that we had welshed on an unspoken agreement which one of us had entered into – oh dread inconsistency! – in all of our names? Would it be said that once again the fully-skimmed cream of the French intelli-gentsia (that is to say, us) had failed in its duty?

No, these things would never be said.

For we decided, in sublime and total accord, that we would concertedly and gently break Karageorgevich's arm, one day when he was on leave, and that then all he'd have to say was that he'd slipped on a banana skin down métro Opéra's long escalator and that, even if no one believed him, he'd be sent to see the regimental psychiatrist, they'd be off his back for a good long while and that the Algerians will probably thrash our hides and that peace has been signed.

And the next day, scarcely had sweet and chubby-fingered dawn dragged, with a deal of difficulty, fellow Phoebus out of bed, than Henri Pollak, a rubbernecked sarge once more, lapping up Paris's ringroad at high speed on his phutting little pedal-assisted engine whose brake-blocks had recently been totally refurbished, went bearing these glad tidings to his fine friend Karawurtz, that is to say that he, Henri Pollak and his personal friends (the personal friends being we) were going to concertedly and gently break his arm next time he was in town and that all he'd have to say was that he'd slipped on a banana skin down the big mechanical diving apparatus in Tourelles métro station and that, even if they didn't believe him, the battalion's psychotherapeutic section would take the matter in hand and that he'd be off the hook for a good long while and that the French have been driven back into the sea, women and children first, the widows sent back to the dowars they came from and the armistice is on the way and peace has been signed.

"Ah, now you're talking," chirruped Karastumpf. "That's a good one." And he was all chuffed up and as pleased as pie.

Meanwhile the rest of us, Henri Pollak's mates, mere rankless civvies, set about arranging the business.

We wrote a splendid letter to a friend who was a doctor in Pau (I should point out at once that he didn't specialize in premature burials, nor was his wife an usherette), and this splendid letter was cagily worded, as a precaution against the Secret Services who had, or so it was claimed, men posted everywhere.

And in this letter we asked this friend who was a doctor

in Pau, though not at all a specialist in premature burials or even having an usherette for a wife, so we asked this doctor friend, in this letter, to send us asap, soonest, by return of post and even pdq, a mind-blasting anaesthetic which was easy to administer and preferably intramuscular.

Then we reckoned that it'd all be a piece of cake. All that'd be necessary, as they say:

Was for him to show us his strapping arm
So that we could do it the utmost harm.

The guy doesn't feel a thing. We trap his arm between the devil and the deep blue sea or, failing that, between two solid planks. We give it a good wrench, he pulls a face, we douse him with booze, we blow his gasket, we leave him to dry off, then there we are: all we have to do is go out into the streets, where the military fraternity is said to muster, proclaiming that he'd slipped on a banana skin down the forty-fold flight of practically century-old steps in métro Pyramides, and even if no one lends us ear, the case'll come under the Brigade's Psychoanalytic Commission, who'll put him out to grass for a while, while the rebels will have gobbled us up raw, negotiations got under way and peace has been signed.

But all we got in way of reply was a nasty note scribbled out by someone whose pen had obviously gone down the wrong way, menacingly exhorting us to look after the bacon that God had sent us, and several exchanges of written exegeses, and dangerously explicit ones at that – but we knew how to live up to our responsibilities when needs must – were required before we received two phials of 7% accelerated Solucrivine, with an enclosed user's manual and a hand-written note of a presumably ironic stamp, pointing out that the gentle breaking of a man's arm wasn't child's play at all, even if several of us went at it at the same time, considering that we risked blowing his bones, his tendons, his synovials, his joints, his fibres, his ligaments, his fatty-tissue, his lymph and the whole carry-on all in one go, and that even if we did manage it, it wouldn't stop the codger from going off to the fields of glory with his arm in a sling plus forty-five days' solitary to boot and that his humero-clastic chums would have the constabulary on their tails till their kingdom comes.

"Pah", we said to one another just like that, and we got Henri Pollak to tell Karakneesup that we were just about all set and Karakneesup got Henri Pollak to tell us that he was just about all set too. And so everyone was just about all set.

But it came to pass at that time, for reasons of which we were to remain in the dark, that Karamel didn't go. Just wasn't in for a tilt. Falempain, good old Falempain, he was in for a tilt, and little Laverrière, he was in for a tilt too, little old Laverrière, warmly nicknamed Ice-Breaker. And even that foul racist Van Ostrack, he was in for a tilt as well. But Karamel just wasn't.

No covered truck watched as he advanced towards itself, wobbling under the weight of Arabicidal paraphernalia. No mustachioed adjutant (with chrome-plated handlebars) inspected his kit, no whimsical captain slipped a white-gloved finger into his stripped-down shooter's grease-gleaming barrel only to draw it out again filthy and remark "it's dirty", no melanophagic, erythrophobic colonel hugged him in his muskular arms, saying "I'm going to miss you, my lad", no bowlegged general let a tear glisten under his eyebrows gone grey from soldiering, while assuring him once more that France and God were counting on them, these Transport Regiments' fine recruits, and that they were brandishing high the sacred torch of western civilization which was in (yellow) peril.

Accordingly, Karabine didn't go and, when he saw his little comrades heading off, a broad grin split his noble features. In the spick-and-span barracks, he stayed on his jack, where he could be seen executing clumsy entrechats with the help of an old broom, or humming the principal arias from *Le Combat de Conflans et d'Honorine*, while scrubbing down the stone-slabbed floor of the above-mentioned.

And, from Saturday night till Sunday evening, he would snuggle his large bonce into the girl he was crazy about's generous head of bronze hair, and whisper sweet versicles to her, as though clouds of Algeria had never darkened the pure sun of his love.

But as far as we, Henri Pollak's mates, were concerned, this was all dead disappointing. Zwounds! There we were all bent over backwards and for nothing, with good cash splashed out for peanuts. What a piss off. As fustration goes, this was fustrating. You're telling me. Friend Henri Pollak could well be a sergeant, but he got what was coming to him, which was a good bollocking, if you pardon my French.

Fortunately, or rather alas, yes, alas, eheu, eheu, hardly two months had gone by by the Gare de Lyon's great clock before the whole set-to started up again in Vincennes's Fort Neuf.

Then the bureaucrats, those lousy shirkers in the Department of Manning Levels, opened their large registers bound in flaming-red cloth and, with their long atrophied Atropos fingers, pointed out the names of those who would soon be off to play soldiers, and on a fine sunny June morning in the year nineteen hundred and something (no names, no dates, begged our friend Henri P. on his knees), the assembled companies were all agog to hear that fateful call-up:

Agave, Alsatian (Germain), Atala (René), Beaulemon, Béret, Blimpe, Bourbon, Bovary, Buonaparte (Max), Burburi, Catalina, Cécédille, Colique, Colin-Clout, Culdesaque, Diego-Suarez, Dostoyewchky, Epaminandate, Flanchet d'Hesperide, Flippe, Funque, Gargoyle, Guzzelle, Harsène, Horgonarhythme, Hospodar, Ignatius-Ignatius, Jacques-Anapes, Jonah, Jujube, Jussieu...

At that moment faint himself felt brave Karadigm. And when his name, which five and half generations of Karadigms had unwittingly borne then handed, gagged and bound, over to him, dropped from Lieutenant Gottisgunne's parson's nose of a mouth, mangling Karadigm (just the name, not the man, alas: a nice distinction from which I shall hey presto set about drawing many an entertaining and mind-boggling digression; but this is a serious moment and I must press on: Oh! Literature! How many torments, how much torture must your sacrosanct love of continuity inflict us with?)...

Where was I? Oh yes. When, then, his name, which five and a half etceteras dropped from Lieutenant Gottisgunne's etcetera, our noble Karachi turned his marvellous damp-eyed gob towards his po-faced pal Pollak (Henri) who, as dry as ever and a sergeant from his head to his boots, slapped him on a charge because it's not done to turn your head when standing to attention.

Nonetheless, that very evening, we were all in the know. Our tanning Henri Pollak had propelled his spluttering velocipede with its turbine and hydraulic suspension at three hundred and ninety-eight hectometres an hour from Vincennes's Fort Neuf to his native Montparnasse where his sweet turtledove was, his lovingly-fitted-out attic, his second selves (that was us, the second selves) and his seventy-five centimetres of Pléiade classics. In such circumstances he didn't even change, but came to meet us clad in khaki, burning to tell us the events to which that day had been witness of: that this time, the goose was cooked, Karalberg was on the list, that he was all put out, that he hadn't even touched his lunch, despite the fact of its having been meatballs, and meatballs are really good, that it was a catastrophey.

And then, wan, yet sublime, we decided to act.

Any reader who wishes to take a break here can. We have, my word, come to what the best authors (Jules Sandeau, Victor Margueritte, Henri Lavedan, even Alain Robbe-Grillet in his latest, *Lenten Christmas*) call a natural turning point.

Let me remind you of the main points which your reader's brains have, or could have, or should have taken on board:

Firstly: that there is an individual named, perhaps approximately, Karathingy, who refuses to go to the Mediterainean (I'm not quite sure about that spelling) the climatic conditions being what they are. In fact we have been rather vague about all that, with a view to weaving little mysteries around our modest tale;

secondly: that there is a group of fine fellows, one of whom I am among, who are as brave as Marignan, as strong as Pathos, as wily as Artemis and as proud as Artaban;

thirdly: that there is a third person, surnamed Pollak and forenamed Henri, ranked sergeant, who seems to spend his life going from the one to the others and from the others to the one, and vice versa, by means of a phutting little moped;

fourthly: that this moped has chrome-plated handlebars;

fifthly: that other individuals, who might be called a supporting cast, wander around between the interstices of the main matter, thus putting it in the limelight, according to those excellent precepts I learnt from the best authors when I was young;

sixthly: that as things stand where we left them, you have the perfect right to wonder: My God, my God, however will it all end?

So, the Algeroclasts gathered up their gear, stacked up their kits, patched up their togs, stitched up their socks, polished up their boots, greased down their guns, drew their rations of Knorr stock-cubes, coffee powder, quinine salts, vermifugal powder, bought in buttons, thread, toothpaste, the works of Camus (Albert), ballpoint pens, Ambre Solaire, boxer-shorts and babouches.

Then the mustachioed adjutant (with chrome-plated handlebars) inspected Karasplotch's outfit; the captain, as switched-on as his switch was long, slid a white-kid-gloved finger into his stripped-down automatic pistol's gleamingly-greased breech to examine its soiled state and ask, in a tone of voice in which insolence strove with perplexity: "Is this what you call a clean automatic pistol?" (but Karasplotch resisted the temptation to reply); the colonel made a long, not overly-foul-mouthed speech for a colonel, from which it emerged firstly that Karasplotch was a dolt and that they were all the same; secondly that he, Colonel Dimbeau, child of arms, son of the regiment, would rather be off to have a bash at Sidi-Belle-Abbesses any day instead of commanding a lot of good-for-nothings like them; thirdly that their sort was more than he could stomach, and fourthly that France had come to a pretty pass.

As for the general, he sent a wire apologizing for not being able to come.

And we rang each other up and realized that the moment had arrived.

On the actual day's actual morning we got up early and in loads of shopping. We bought some wine, lots of wine, because we were going to be thirsty, and then we bought some rice, olives, anchovies, eggs and charcutery, because we were also going to be hungry, and, since it wouldn't do to be stingy and the least we could do would be to pour some oil on good old Karathingy's troubled waters, before pouring some onto his dislocated shoulder or dangling humerus, we also bought in cakes, sweets, candy, dainties, fruit and spirits.

Then we bought hypodermic needles, the corresponding syringes, cotton wool, lint, eleven metres of Elastoplast, safety pins, pliers, a gag, a jack and two francs' worth of carpet tacks which might come in handy, all from the large bazaar at the corner of rue Boris-Vian and boulevard Teilhard-de-Chardin, just opposite the metro exit, next to the butcher's.

During the afternoon, we did the housework, because the place was a real tip and we could hardly receive a mate whose cubitus we were going to unscrew in a real tip.

And as we all knuckled down, everything was soon ready: the flat was gleaming, the bottles lined up on the mantelpiece, the meal needed but a gesture from us to spring forth onto the ready-laid table (one of the things we were proudest of, between you and me: it was a rustic table, evidently little-used to large urban areas' vibrant civilization; from its country background, it had kept a sometimes worrying penchant for the nomadic life; initially, it had shown us a stubborn, mute, yet horribly effective hostility and it had taken us almost six months, six months of patience, of cajolling, of firmness – but, reassure yourselves, we never beat it about – to have it obey us, remain once and for all in its place and stay still while we laid it).

It was ten to six. The wind went chill. We shut the windows then plunged joyfully into a perusal of our large encyclopædia's article on "Fractures and Diverse Complications" to get genned up concerning the business on which we'd soon have to talk about.

At six o'clock, our good friend Hubert turned up with a blow torch, which he had borrowed eleven months previously. He said:

"Well, well, isn't the place neat!"

We answered:

"We're expecting Karasplash."

He said that we could count him in and suggested going out to get some gin, which met our hearty approval. He went down and soon came back up again with Lucien in tow, whom, said he, he had met on the way.

And Lucien phoned up his Emilie, and Hubert phoned up his sis, and we phoned up the Draculas, who were out, the Baguepaipes, who said they'd come, and big Blerot who always made us laugh, but of whom we could not get hold.

And our mates came in such a crowd that it was just as if we were at Vendôme, the day *The Umbrellas of Cherbourg* opened (the kind reader will surely pardon us this slight anachronism). And, as everyone wasn't in the know, those that were in the know put those that weren't yet in the know in the know.

And then – this was inevitable – some of them said that we must be out of our trees to reckon – even for a moment – on breaking Karalahari's arm, that it was bloody dangerous, that if we gave him the jab he wouldn't feel a thing, then it wouldn't just be his arm we'd break, but we'd also rupture his synovials, pop his joints, rip his tendons, disincrust his filaments, caramelize his ligaments and the rest of the carry-on.

That (what is more) the military doctors would only have to give the most casual glance at his supposed injury in order to see right through the ridiculous plot that had perpetrated it and that, following this, the above-mentioned Karagrunt would leave notwithstanding, with his arm in plaster and sixty days' solitary for good measure, while we, his unfortunate accomplices, would have the gendarmerie on our tracks unto the eleventh generation.

"So what?" we chorused in unison and with one voice, whilst giving each other questioning glances.

Thereupon, the chairman of the meeting declared the temporary dissolution of the General Assembly and ordered the constitution of three commissions which would sit *in camera*, one in the kitchen, the other in the bedroom, the third in the main Committee room, the which commissions would be sovereign and ventripotent and informed of the various projects as they came under the Secretary's jurisdiction, who would relay the said projects to them after their inscription in the minutes, reserving only unto himself the right to decide their attribution (a procedural ploy which fooled no one and further delayed the commencement of any real debate).

After a few amendments, motions, attachments, points of order, drafts, counter-drafts, interruptions, cavils, threatened walkouts and other assorted incidents, the main propositions concerning Karakulchie's immediate future were finally reduced to five, on which we voted with clenched fists and raised hands.

The first one reckoned that come what may Karakrack's arm should be broken in any case for, it was emphasized, that is why we were there. This formalistic proposition unleashed 9% of the assembly's enthusiasm, which was over the top.

The second favoured our pushing of a dead-drunk Karavanne downstairs; Nature, it was claimed, would do the rest: a disgustingly ideological notion which the wily neurophysiologist in me put paid to in four seconds flat by demonstrating that the proverb: "There is a God of drunkards" has a firm scientific basis, which did not stop the said motion from gaining 13% of the votes.

The third saw the only solution in his taking up a strident political stance: a courageous Karanette loudly and, if possible, intelligibly proclaims that he is against this filthy war and lies down by some filthy railway tracks until some filthy level-crossing keepers come along and beat him into a filthy mess. This rascally but, it must be admitted, not unhumorous proposition was much discussed given that it made better sense for us to have official hands do the dirty work, which would leave us mere cowards; which we were at a rate of only 23%.

The fourth proposition suggested that Karatishoo should fall ill, preferably seriously, and proposed a choice between tuberculosis, jaundice, double phlegmon and advanced rickets. This picked up a quarter of the group's agreement.

Finally, the fifth proposition was that Karakiri should go bonkers. This appealed to 37% of us.*

---

* The wary reader who adds up the total may find that it exceeds 100%. He would be quite right in deducing that some people voted twice.

And so it was decided that, under our kindly guidance and with the help of the wonderful results currently derivable from militant psychopathology's data, Karasteria would fake an auto-suicide attempt and get discharged for rampant schizophrenia, or else paranoia simplex.

The particular friend of ours (everything had been foreseen) who was doing third-year pharmacology (he still is, by the way, and he's just got married; he's got eleven children, all boys, all lovely, all healthy: isn't life funny...) went off home to fetch his codex so as to look up some drug we could get from the chemist's which Karaswellin could gulp down his fill of without any (or not much) real danger, albeit without any pleasure.

At last, at the stroke of a quarter to nine, while despair with its crooked fingers and gnashing of teeth had started to invade the place, Karajoan made his warmly applauded entrance. His superior in rank, that noble and generous Henri Pollak came in first, dressed up in his Sunday best: a wine-dark V-neck sweater, a burgundy tee-shirt, ultramarine kegs and black basketball boots with strass ornamentation; while your Karajoan cut a fine figure of a soldier, in his soldierly outfit, in his khaki tunic with frogs and hoops likewise, his kepi cheekily perched askew on his sinciput and his huge hobnailed clodhoppers which screeched across our freshly polished parquet. Coming in to a boisterous welcome, he felt intimidated. We made some room for him. And he felt the whole gang's friendly stares fall upon him.

Karastein was an individual whose slender build did not spoil a certain burliness. From toe to tip he measured, at a rough guess, a good six feet. His overall width was around twenty-eight inches. His chest capacity was quite phenomenal, his heart-beat slow, his looks agreeable. His face lacked any distinguishing characteristic: he had two blue eyes, a splendid nose, a large mouth, two sticky-out ears and a rather grubby neck. With no beard or moustache we'd have spotted him at once. With his abundant bushy eyebrows, his sensual nostrils, his chubby cheeks, his full lips, his strong chin, his square jaw, his low forehead, his balding temples and his witty eyelids. However, his dumb-show expressiveness did seem limited. He looked about as intelligent as the native to whom Arthur de Bougainville asked his way after alighting at the Gare de Lyon on September 11th, 1908.

And if we add that he was naturally taciturn, that he looked lost in a daydream, that his hair had just been cut by some talentless barber and that he was wringing and re-wringing his coarsely grained kepi in his fat hairy hands we can suppose that a sufficiently precise portrait of this man has been painted so that should you ever run into him at the corner of rue Boris-Vian and boulevard Teilhard-de-Chardin you will rapidly change pavements, just as we ourselves would if a similar mishap befell us (but, of course, we know how the story ends...).

These rare elements along with the whispered scraps which Sergeant (with chrome-plated handlebars) Henri Pollak had managed to pass on to us between front and living-room doors led us to believe that, a priori, Karavage was a simple soul, whose mould had since been broken, possessed of quite extraordinary physical strength (had he not broken our one and only wicker chair just by sitting on it?), whose wits were slightly off the average and whose faith in the social norms of his tribe of origin was just about instinctive; we had no intention of delving any deeper into these inductions, given that not one of us could give a damn.

Some pre-dinner drinks were served. Those thirsty ones among us who were as numerous as we were (in fact, have I said that there was a good dozen of us?) got stuck in to them as fast as poverty in the world or gonorrhoea in the lower orders of the Breton clergy. But Karalepiped didn't serve himself. He sat there, with his snot-filled nostrils, not daring to blow his nose, curled up in the corner, not breathing a word, unless, egged on by the convergence of our friendly gazes, he would sketch a feeble smile and say, deadpan: "Nice place you've got here, anyway, small, but nice." Which as dead on goes, was dead on.

We finally sat down to eat. Bout time too. And what a crush! First we ate some sardines with bread and butter. After that, we drank some white wine, which was pretty classy stuff, for sure. After that we had braised saucisson from chez Pétras, on the rue Volta, which is worth all the braised saucissons in the world. Then a large platter of rice appeared with great pomp and circumstance, garnished with many an olive as well as anchovy fillets arranged in quincunxes, alternating with little heaps of thinly-sliced cucumbers, themselves flanked by shelled shrimps, the whole being deliciously covered by a scattering of finely-chopped peppers, capers and hard-boiled egg yolks, as yellow as buttercups.

And Henri Pollak, as the truly-soldierly sergeant that he had been for the past fifteen and a bit months, opened, one after the other, three bottles of ageless Château-Bercy red, putting his index finger into his mouth and, using his cheek as a soundboard, going: "Pop, pop, pop", while others gave signs of general hihilarity by clicking their tongues, raising their caps, waggling their heads and twiddling their mustaches.

After the meal, we conveyed ourselves to the lounge, where coffee was served, cigars and cigarettes offered round and various spirits passed back and forth.

And to get Karafalk relaxed we tried to get him chatting and on the spur of the moment asked him point-blank what he thought about the war, whether he was for or against it. The reader may well remember how popular this question was at the time and how hardly a day would pass by without its inspiring either private or public debate. But we had quite a particular reason for asking it here: that is, as the ever-attentive reader has no doubt noticed, since we have not missed out, Heaven forfend, on chucking in as if by chance the odd wicked and sometimes even devilish reference to the matter, that is, I repeat, that we were rather put out about having to compromise ourselves with an individual who wasn't even politicked; we felt bad about putting ourselves out to save the peace for someone who just wanted to sleep sweetly between the girl he was crazy about's sheets, while his best pals stood guard-duty outside institutions in danger of losing their honour, and who seemed to allot only a limited, indeed piffling, importance to Liberty, to Democracy, to Human Ideals, to Socialism and the rest of the carry-on.

But unfortunately for us, who might here have found the makings of a fine apologue, Karatledge wasn't as thick as he looked. Aware of this misleading personality trait, he made an effort to rise to the occasion and said precisely what we wanted to get him to say while hoping that he wouldn't, that is to say, that he agreed with us, that he too was the sort of bloke who, in other circumstances and if asked nicely, would have "carried his case" and turned his coat.

But in any case, when it came down to it, was it really necessary to take such risks to get at the purely political side of the business? Wasn't it enough to be quite simply a fine fellow, a good old soul, a humble, little, fine, neighbourhood personage who buys his morning paper in his slippers, who doesn't like war, cos war's nasty, who likes peace, cos peace's neat, who likes going dancing on Sunday nights in the public square to an accordeon playing *Nini peau de chien* under tricolour fairylights? And what about love! Wasn't having a girl he was crazy about reason enough to be saved?

When this theoretical absolution had doubtlessly won Karagandhi round, he finally got round to opening up a bit. He confided in us that he was a worker, that he wasn't happy in the army and that he'd never seen so many books before.

So immediately we, being the popularizers that we were, bitten by the enlightenment propaganda bug, we who would have liked to have been school teachers in a small Savoy village at the end of the nineteenth century, so that we could have got little peasants in smocks to read Rousseau, Voltaire, Vallès and Zola, handed him a whole batch: *Moby Dick*, the *Volcano* (Ah! the *Volcano*! Old Popo! Qaqahuaq! Sé gousta hesté hhrrarrdin'! Mescalito per favor! What a book!), *The Crisis of European Consciousness* (and why not? I know your game, you damned misopaedists! Obscurantists!), Henry Miller – we liked Henry Miller at the time – Gaston Leroux (he hadn't even read Gaston Leroux!) and others too which were cluttering up the place. But he very nicely turned them down, saying that, maybe, when peace had returned, when he had the chance to read these works in comfort, when he could savour them to their very marrow, then, yes. But not, he added, this evening, no, this evening his heart just wasn't in it.

This long speech's carefully chosen phraseology allowed

us to fully evaluate the harmful influence which Sergeant Henri Pollak, our very own mate (and we were sorry for him)'s sophisticated culture had had on this young soul; his long speech left him drained. He almost collapsed and slumped into a hostile muteness. Heavy silence hung over the smoke-filled room. And the sad thought came to us that it was finished, that Karastenberger had given us a good giggle with his big boots, his cheery mug, his slowish wits, his good will and his stammer, but that now the ball was in our court, that we'd have to make up our minds about getting him out of the mess he was in, and that things were going to turn nasty any moment now.

So our clan's chief mandarin and venerable egg-head wiped his glasses, took his pipe out of his mouth and spoke as follows:

"Well, my old chap, we've given your story a deal of thought. And it's no laughing matter. All the same, one mustn't play silly buggers. We'd be only too pleased to gently break your arm, but it'd be damned dangerous, follow me? After the jab, you won't feel a thing, and we could well wind up decoupling your joints, popping your synovials, snapping your ligaments and your intra-articulatory tendons. And what's more, old chap, you mustn't take your army doctors for cunts. They're not so easily fooled. Never take people for cunts, that's what the army doctors'll say and, my old chap, all this won't stop your going off on manoeuvres with your arm in a sling and a kick up the rearguard, with ninety days in the cooler to boot, or even a court martial, the glasshouse, borstal, the full whack, while we, the cats' paws, will have the police on our arses for decades on end, follow me?"

"Alack! Alack!" (went the other) "We be Cursenfolk as good as your zelfe! I shall goon chuck meself straight in the Seine, hey presto, let's get it over with, by jolly old jingo I will!"

"Calm it, friend, calm it," said the gathering's apparent leader, twiddling his bicycle chain in what was supposed to be a threatening manner. "Don't let's panic. During the discussions which your case has given rise to, it has transpired that your falling mentally ill wouldn't be a bad idea: you swallow a few pills, get into a bit of a state, no longer know what you're about, they make you sick it all up, it looks as if you wanted to go west, everyone knows the army doesn't like that, because it's bad for company morale, so off you'll go to see the psychiatrist, you get demobbed, then you're laughing."

The idea that he was going to commit harikiri within the next four hours didn't seem to go down unduly well with our friend (or rather with Henri Pollak's friend. Let's be clear. Henri Pollak's friends are not necessarily our friends. Thank God) Karawhine. He even had a good moan about it. But what can I say? There were not only more of us, but we were also smarter: the seminar we had attended for two consecutive years on door-to-door salesmanship, run by the Sixth Section of Higher Studies, proved indispensable: by dint of browbeating arguments, glasses of calvados and brandy, wily syllogisms and brilliant off-the-cuff remarks, it took us less than a hundred and thirteen minutes (we had come across harder nuts to crack) to work up his enthusiasm and he wound up reckoning that it wasn't such a bad idea after all: yes, why not, yes, he was going to take a few little pills, line his stomach with barbiturates, then have a nice sleepy-byes. Then he'd wake up in a hospital bed, with a little tube in his mouth, half a dozen buckets at his feet,

and a few male military nurses (another bunch of lousy
shirkers) who would be patting his back, and then he'd go
and see the trick-cyclists, he'd do his pieces, he'd tell them
that he wasn't stable
that sometimes he was fed up with life
that he wanted to blow his brains out
that he'd rather chuck himself in the river
that he was fed up with life
that sometimes he wanted to chuck himself in the river
that he wanted to blow his brains out
that he wasn't stable
that he'd rather get it over with once and for all
that he was so depressed you just wouldn't believe it it was
like a hole
a black hole
a big black hole
brrr
he'd had it with existence
(what was the point of going on)
he was scared and it wasn't right
he wasn't stable
he'd rather chuck himself in the river
whatever, he'd get them to understand that if there was one
headcase in the regiment, then he was it, and that Captain
Terminal's bouts of dribbling masperoclastics were small
beer compared with what he had. And the trick-cyclists
would diagnose a nice little case of paranoia simplex, or
maybe even that he was schizo, and they'd send him to hospital, he wouldn't go to those craggy mountains and maybe
the Algerians would finally win their bloody war and that the
cease-fire will come into force and that peace has been signed.

Upon which, a deeply emotional Karamega downed a
large glass of gin and started chuckling to himself.

He spent the next hour dozing like a baby while others of whom we were among set about saving his military skin by looking up in the codex what substance he was going to stuff himself with:

curare was adjuged to be, all things taken into account, inefficacious;
Acheronate of Atropos was forbidden for troopers and non-comms in reserves;
liquid extract of Tædium Vitae: cost the earth;
and we fell back on Dr Mortibus's Soluble Camphorated Thanatine:

Nicotate of Methilda · · · · · · · · · · · · · · 0.005
8-Chlorotheophyllinate-dimethyl-amino-ethyl-
benzhydryl ether · · · · · · · · · · · · · · · · 0.1
Paradichlorobenzene · · · · · · · · · · · · · · 0.4
Londinium · · · · · · · · · · · · · · · · · · 0.1
Quinquina succirubra · · · · · · · · · · · · · 0.8
James Bond · · · · · · · · · · · · · · · · · · 0.07
Agrippa dobignia · · · · · · · · · · · · · · traces
Placebo-excipient · · · · · · · · quant suff (98.5%)

a little known compound but one which no one never, it seemed, had ever complained about never. Henri Pollak, a methodical fellow, noted down this drug's characteristics in his modern man's diary, with its loose leaves (and chrome-plated catch) upon which we decided, in the first place, to wake Karasweiszer up as expeditiously as we could, to get him back onto his feet and to dress him in his most bootiful raiment;
secondly, to frog march him down to the nearest of our neighbourhood chemists (that is, at the junction of rue Boris-Vian and boulevard Teilhard-de-Chardin), to buy him,

despite his fishy stare, a tube of Dr Ad. Patres's Soluble Camphorated Thanatine, to generously get him a cup of coffee at the counter of the café over the road, and there to watch over his massive – but not excessive – ingurgitation of these small hypnofic, somnitive and dormigenic tablets; thirdly, to take him to a hotel and wish him a long and good night;

and, small *d*, not to miss catching up with his news as soon as ever we might.

Afterwards, we reckoned, the goose is cooked, easy as pie. All that was needed, as they say, was

That he has a barbiturate snooze
For him his psydekick wits to lose.

The geezer drops off like a log. His bits and bobs have been nicely laid out. On the bedside table he has left a photograph of the girl he's crazy about, the bitter pills' jettisoned tube, a half-drunk glass, a letter which states straight out that he is fed up with life, that he doesn't want to go to Algeria, that he has taken twelve tablets of Dr Kadaver's thanatine, that he begs his dad's forgiveness, his colonel's, his mum's, his captain's who had always been so good to him, his adjutant's who he would never be angry with again even though he'd given him eight days once when he hadn't done a thing he swore it, his sarge Henri Pollak's who had always been a true pal, good old Falempain's (but good old Falempain was already three weeks dead) and lime Laverrière who was warmly nicknamed Ice-Breaker.

And in the pale light of dawn, the hotelier with his hangdog looks and rumpled features, concerned about the fate of that strange traveller who had been wearing the uniform of the glorious French army (the best, because the best-selling), would hammer on the above-mentioned's door, would, with the bellowing of a calf being slaughtered, raise up the neighbours, the plain-clothes police, the CID, the RSPCA, the VSOP, the morgue, the President's office, the *Figaro*, the emergency services, and the slumbering Karaschmurz would be off to carry on his ravaging snooze on a hospital cot's feathery mattress and would only wake up when he had forty-three centimetres of disinfected tubing down his œsophagus (or else down his pharynx). Eleven (or maybe even down his larynx), eleven (or down his trachea, what do I know about it?), eleven (you might say that if I don't know anything about it, then I'd better leave off writing: if you want to write, then you have to have the vocabulary for it. Perhaps true, but I'm quite sure you don't know any more than I do about such things. In any case, you'd never be able to write this story in my place!) eleven (let's just say that he'll have forty-three centimetres of disinfected tubing down his throat and leave it at that...) eleven hand-picked psycolonels (then) would take his pulse, look at his tongue, evaluate his intellect, look under his toes to check how his Babinski reflex was (Ah-ah! I've got you there: I'm quite sure you don't know what a Babinski reflex is, and don't think I'm going to tell you) and, sickened, would pack him off into storage while the brave moujahidin turn the tables on us and a truce is due any day now and peace has been signed.

Accordingly was it accomplished: while the bulk of the gang stayed behind to polish off the bottles, Henri Pollak, that brave Henri Pollak and another (whose name would mean nothing to you) took Karabougar under his armpits and off for a stroll.

Time fugit. 'Twas late. Some of them dozed off on the floor. Some snuck away on cats' paws, others fell over the bottles and started cursing their creator's name, while others still went into the kitchen to eat the cheese. Women in black veils knelt before the icon, crossed themselves and prayed for the soldier's safety. While, totally indifferent, Lester Young, accompanied by John Lewis on the piano, Paul Chambers on bass and Kenny Clarke on drums, played something very simple and very beautiful (*Blue Star*, Norman Granz, no. 6933) on the muted electrophone.

At the stroke of about three or a quarter past, Henri Pollak and his companion (whose name would mean nothing to you)'s reappearance caused a stir. Those of us that still had the strength to speak lifted ourselves up on our elbows and asked how it had gone.

They launched into such a complicated tale that the infamous dictation set by Claude Simon for candidates to the entry examinations for *L'Ecole Normale Supérieure* of Childminding (sole session of 195_) would have seemed in comparison more straight forward than Isaac de Benserade's (1613–1691) celebrated hexastich in which clarity vies with gracefulness and which I cannot resist the temptation of quoting in full:

> *Between the Cake and Eating It*
> *My Heart does not know Which to choose:*
> *For if I have the Cake*
> *Then I shall not Eat It;*
> *And yet if I Eat It*
> *I shall not have the Cake.*

(The authenticity of these verses is perhaps doubtful. I shall not come down on one side or the other, but rather limit myself to pointing out that this hexastich has, like all others, its regulatory six lines and that, *sed etiam*, its structure, imagery, texture and style are indubitably priceless; if its meaning is far from clear, then this is the fault of Allegory, which travels badly; anyway, let's agree that it's a pretty little thing).

Right. So, Henri Pollak and the other one (whose name would mean nothing to you) had dragged Karastinck into a chemist's in Montparnasse (where, will the reader please recall to yourself, one of these three nyctobates had first seen the light of day), they'd weighed him, just for the hell of it, then bought him for his own personal use a small, greenish, indeed rather lugubrious tube containing twelve mauve, oval-shaped tablets.

Then they had entered a lugubrious café and had asked the barman, whose oval-shaped head, greenish tinge and off-mauve apron were just like something out of a Vincente Minnelli film, had, anyway, asked the barman for three black, very black coffees and the barman had brought them three black, black as Indian ink is black, coffees. So, Henri Pollak, unless it was the other one, whose name would mean nothing to you (anyway, you're better off not knowing who it was), had put four tablets into what was to be Karabloom's cup, along with eleven lumps of sugar, had given it a good stir with a little spoon which had come out half-eaten thro, had raised the cup to Karacalla's lips, who knocked it back in one, and had then patted him on his back till he'd brought up his wind.

Following this, Henri Pollak (our friend) and his confederate (whose name would still mean nothing to you) had dictated a letter to Karaschwein which stated that Karaschwein was so fed up with life that it was incredible, that he wasn't particularly sold on the idea of going off fine-toothcombing the jebels, that he had taken twelve of Dr Morty Kohl's mauve thanatine tablets, that Sergeant Henri

Pollak had had absolutely nothing to do with it; that he begged his dad's forgiveness, his mum's, his colonel's, his captain's who was a peach of a man, his adjutant's who had shown his mettle, his pals Laverrière's and Falempain's (but Falempain had already had a red hole in his right side for the past three weeks) and General de Gaul, the President of the French Republic's.

Karapuffy read it, reread it, signed it in his childish hand and brought up some more wind. He looked exhausted and trembled like a young shoot caressed by Zephyrs. His face had gone a worrying-looking colour, the end of his nose was turning pink and his scalp starting to bald. Henri Pollak and the other one, whose name would mean nothing to you, reckoned it was time to be off.

They searched hotels but found no beds were free. These things happen.

They walked for ages, such ages that they finally got tired and stopped. And Karafield, without a word of warning, slumped into the guttress and started to snore.

"Well we can't just leave him here," said Henri Pollak.

"Indeed not," said the other one, whose name wouldn't tell you a thing.

"Well, well, well," Henri Pollak emphasized.

"It's as plain as your face," said the other one, whose name would mean very little to you.

Encouraged by this total agreement, they stared into the whites of each other's eyes and, cogitating in unison, had a quick brainstorming session, from which the following luminous pensée emerged: since there was no room at the inn, Karacass would have to go back to the barracks.

No sooner said than done: Karabiniere was put back onto his feet, pushed into a taxi, which happened to be passing and into which Henri Pollak and the other one (whose name would mean nothing to you, honestly) likewise dived, and the taxi transjogged them at high speed to the gates of Vincennes's Fort Neuf, following a short itinerary which Henri Pollak knew well, since he took it morning and night on his phutting little moped with its telescopic fork (and easy-to-read oil gauge).

Then (and only then) they woke up Karasnooze by setting fire to little bits of wood stuck in his ears, and they told him to run off quickly to bed, to take the four mauve thanatine tablets which they smilingly placed in his hand, to put the letter somewhere conspicuous next to his helmet and to wait confidently for what would happen next. And they also told him that he didn't owe them a penny, not for the tablets, nor for the coffee, nor for the taxi (this was true great-heartedness), that they'd been only too pleased to do him a good turn and that, as our beautiful country's journeymen put it:

> *If they had to take it, then*
> *They'd take that same old road again.*

Upon which, managing to conceal what they were up to, but not their state of mind, they chucked Karabesque out of that venal jollopy and gave directions to its driver to take them back the way they'd come. And, as they passed over the Seine, Henri Pollak, with the noble gesture of a sower of seeds, chucked the four remaining tablets into the dark waters, which swallowed them up.

And God, who sees all, saw that all that was not going to serve much purpose.

And there we are, said we, he's gone. We had another drink. Henri Pollak went to bed, then the others. We hit the hay.

43

The next day we tidied up. A bomb had hit the place. We washed up the plates, the knives, the forks, the glasses and the ashtrays. We threw out the empties and scrubbed down the parquet.

At the stroke of four, a few mates dropped by.

"So," they asked. "What about Karameraman? What happened to Karameraman?"

"Fuck knows," said we, adding: "Have to wait for our Henri Pollak."

Our Henri Pollak kept us waiting for a long time. He turned up at the stroke of seven, all skin and bones, his head like a cauliflower, his face twitching all over, his tie tied badly round his long badly-cooked chicken's neck and his Adam's apple bobbling up and down spasmodically.

"So," said we. "What about Karavioli?"

"Oh no, oh no," moaned Henri Pollak, "don't talk to me about it, don't talk to me about it."

And, after a sip of melissa water, told us what had happened:

That very morning, when our great and dear friend Sergeant Pollak (Henri), still hardly over the emotions of the night before and with his guts all in a turmoil from the four sorts of spirits with which he had been foolish enough to mix, had melancholically straddled his scooter with its fretwork pedals, had left his native Montparnasse, where dwelt his promised one, his bridal suite, his page-boys and wedding presents, had, heavy with sleep, driven through Fort Neuf's gates, had saluted the guard and all that,
wha–
(but firstly I would advise the reader, indeed could hardly counsel him too strongly to reread, certainly the entire text,

but especially the above clause and to admire its barbarity: this implicit self-criticism will do for the rest of it).

So what had our Henri Pollak seen in the barracks yard? A moped with chrome-plated handlebars? No, not at all! You're not even warm. He, our own Pollak, had seen with his own eyes tarpaulined trucks, fine tarpaulined trucks waiting to be filled up with merry men to take them away to the railway station. And what else had our Henri Pollak seen? A mope-? Of course not, you complete cretin! He had seen, seen with his own eyes, wending his way towards those tarpaulined trucks, bent double under his arabicidal burden's paraphernalia, or rather paraphernalia's burden, his eyes puffy, his skin yellow, looking a complete twat, the great Karathustra, the true Karathustra and the only Karathustra.

Our poor Henri Pollak had gone up to him and said:

"Hey, Karawhatnees, whatcha doing here for Chrissake?"

"Ah shut up," that rude (and ungrateful, and wicked) Karapoplektick had said.

Our poor Henri Pollak couldn't get another word out of him. But since this Henri Pollak of ours was perseverance made flesh, he set about sussing things out. He quizzed the blokes in the barracks room, the guardsmen, the rubber-necks, the neighbours, the janitors, and, half deducing (for he had a bit of nous did Henri Pollak), half imagining (for he also had a bit of an imagination, and a good bit too, did Henri Pollak), he managed to work out what his fine and generous friend's last hours in Vincennes must have been.

It thus transpired that early in the morning of the above-mentioned day, being perhaps afraid of hitting the hay without knowing what was going to happen next, this Karatwit had got it into his little noddle to chase away his alcoholic vapours and nightbirds by going for a stroll in the nearby woods, instead of going to bed in the strict sense of the term. The guardpost had seen him directing his loxodromic steps towards the high-hills of avenue Gustave-Gesselaire. An hour later, the look-out had seen him come back and suddenly collapse. With unthinking bravery, the guard had gone to wake him up and, as soon as he was shaken, Karabamboo had thought nothing of relieving himself of three-quarters of a litre of gin, a good quarter of a litre of rum, the same of marc brandy, a little less of calvados, a few sucked lemon slices, enough rice to keep the population of China happy and a few other substances among which some mauve oval-shaped molecules of a highly dormitive nature still doubtlessly swam, the whole lot going over the guardsman's freshly ironed breeches, which rather put him out. An emergency despatch rider was summoned and sent to raise the fire-picket, which sent back its best corporal who put Karalysis back onto his feet, gave him a vigorous dressing-down and sent him to bed without any pudding.

And, in the pale light of dawn, Karalina went back to the grey barracks room. He collapsed fully dressed onto the bed, with his feet on the pillow and his head propped on his helmet and started to snore as though that was the only thing he'd ever learnt how to do.

Three hours later, the band of the Republican Guard, who had come to give the garrison commander an aubade on the occasion of his niece Caroline's name-day, burst into the overture from *The Magic Flute*, segued rapidly into the Polka in F from *The Thieving Magpie* and finished up (con brio) with the *Delirious Symphony* by Frederic Brafort. Karacrack got up, had a good wash and brush up, got his stuff together, then pissed off like everyone else.

Which proves, if proof be needed, that discipline is the true driving-force of armies.

And that was that, as the best authors say to make it clear that things are well and truly over.

"Phew!" we all went. "Yup," said Henri Pollak.

"Lawdy, lawdy," said a third.

In truth, we felt like crying.

"This isn't that at all," we all said after a long and pregnant pause. "Where is old Karanoia right now? He can't be there yet, surely?"

We learnt from Henri Pollak, the horse's mouth, that trains full of Algeroclasts left long after nightfall from a station, set by for that sole and unique purpose, in some backwoods near Versailles.

Poor Karadine! He who thought he was going to stay and sleep sweetly between the girl he was crazy about's arms, and that he would never go to cross those rocky crags, now it turned out that he was perhaps in that train, all alone and as sad as can be. We thought about the war, over there, in the hot sun: the sand, the stones and the ruins, the cold awakenings under canvas, the forced marches, battles of ten against one, war, in fact.

War ain't no picnic, indeed it ain't. In truth, we felt like crying (I think I've already said that).

And so we said to one another all of a suddenly:

"Better go for a look-see." And off we went arm in arm behind Sergeant Henri Pollak. We took the train to Versailles. We brought in loads of goodies: cigarettes, cigars, half a bottle of whisky, sweets, chocolate creams, an embroidered scarf, colour magazines, paperbacks and a set of little lucky-charms which could suit a variety of occasions. We decided to give him our photos and addresses so that he could write to us when he was over there, to send him food-parcels and to be his wartime sponsors.

> *Once on a night both luminous and fine*
> *Amid the dark forest's gigantic glades*
> *Forty carriages stood there in a line*
> *Crammed to bursting with geezers and grenades.*

> *With so many men who'd know what to do?*
> *Who'd know what to do with so many men?*
> *The first class was full, the second class too*
> *As though all of France Herself was there then.*

> *A few old civvies, a pa and two mas,*
> *Dried their bright eyes which were swimming with tears*
> *And, as the odd soldier pissed on the cars,*
> *They said their good-byes to their little dears.*

> *While other pranksters were plucking guitars,*
> *Some head-strong gangs were chorusing ditties;*
> *And drafting officers passed round cigars*
> *While wine-sad drunkards trembled with DTs.*

> *And boozers burped in each other's faces;*
> *And inspired thinkers piously wrote*
> *Pages to tell the ills of their cases;*
> *And paratroop vicars grinned and took note.*

> *Over the train the night was all balmy,*
> *The loco-emotive all set to go,*
> *Vict'ry shone in the eyes of the army:*
> *Are stations the only place without woe?*

We looked for ages and ages. We went up and down the

train, first in one direction, then in the other. We tried getting into the carriages, but this wasn't allowed. So, at each compartment we yelled:

"Oi, Karaphrenick! You there? Show yourself then! It's your mate, Henri Pollak!"

"There's no Kara-whatever-you-said here," is all we got in reply. Or else we were told to:

"Shut yer bleeding mouth!"

We then faced up to the fact that either Karadoodledoo wasn't on this particular train, or else he didn't want to speak to us.

Then Henri Pollak and the rest of us headed back home along the Versailles road. We took the train back to Les Invalides. We shared out the paperbacks, the cigarettes and the chocolates. We went for a drink on the terrace of Le Select and polished off the half-bottle of whisky. Then everyone went home. And we never heard hide nor hair of that rapscallion again.

INDEX

of the ornamentations and flowers of rhetoric or, to be more precise, of the metabolas and parataxes which the author believes he has identified in the text which you have just read.

THE EXETER TEXT: JEWELS, SECRETS, SEX

Perec

THE EXETER TEXT
Jewels, Secrets, Sex

Renderer: E. N. Menk

LEXESPHERE PRESS
New Engleterre

INTRODUCTION

DAVID BELLOS

The Exeter Text was written during a short holiday at Blévy, the weekend home of Perec's adoptive family, in 1972, and was published the following autumn.

In 1967, Perec became a member of OuLiPo, a group of writers and mathematicians concerned with the literary potential of formal constraints or "writing with rules". With a radio play in German, *Die Maschine* (1968) and then, most famously, with the lipogrammatic novel, *A Void* (1969), Perec had become the acknowledged champion of writing done under the hardest of rules. *The Exeter Text* is most obviously a complement or reciprocal to *A Void*: whereas the latter avoids all and any words containing the commonest letter in the alphabet, *The Exeter Text* uses none of the vowels except *e*.

In order to write a four-fold lipogram, avoiding the letters *a*, *i*, *o* and *u*, Perec obtained the permission of OuLiPo to make one specified change to French spelling, and to be allowed to make such further changes as he needed as the text progressed. These liberties make *The Exeter Text* a different kind of exercise from *A Void*, which observes the standard rules of the French language with only occasional and virtually unnoticeable exceptions. The "retern of the e?"

does the opposite: it bends and twists spelling rules with unrivalled inventiveness. It is as much an exercise in *how far you can go* in orthographic incorrectness – without losing the reader– as a strict exercise on an alphabetic trapeze.

Perec was in the middle of a long-drawn out course of analysis with J.-B Pontalis when he wrote *The Exeter Text*, which is just about the only one of his works to deal explicitly with sex. However, it is equally probable that the language game being played – an exercise with increasingly improper spellings and vocabulary – drew or drove the writer into fantastical improprieties that he hints at almost nowhere else in his work.

The story told in *The Exeter Text* is also a loose and humorous transposition of a family myth. During the German Occupation of France, Georges Perec's uncle, David Bienenfeld, entrusted a stock of pearls and jewels to a travelling salesman, who was to take it across the demarcation line and return the package to the family once it too had reached the Free Zone, whence it was still possible for Jews to escape from Nazi-occupied Europe, and to make their way to America. The family myth alleges that the salesman, who was homosexual, organized a transvestite party once he got to Marseilles. He bedecked his companions with the Bienenfeld jewels for the evening, but the partygoers made off at the end of the orgy before changing back into male attire – and took the jewels with them. Thus the stock with which a new jewellery business would have been built disappeared, and whatever plans the family had for reaching America were shelved. *The Exeter Text* does not reveal any secrets of family history: but the British setting of this linguistically and sexually outrageous novella may owe something to the inherited story, which can serve as one (amongst many) explanations of why Perec became a writer in French and not English.

NOTE

The original of the sonnet on page 92 was by Adolphe Haberer.

The epigraph is taken from a three-page text, entitled "Eve's Legend" by Henry Richard Vassal-Fox, third Lord Holland. It was published in the 1836 *Keepsake*.

RULES

1. The word "and" may be spelt 'n'.
2. The letter "y" when consonantal (e.g. "yes") will be permitted, as will the semi-vowel "y" in digraphs such as "they"; only the full vowel (e.g. "gypsy") will be disallowed.
3. Various distortions will be gradually accepted as the text progresses; no list of them can possibly be given here.

E SERVEM LEX EST, LEGEMQVE TENERE NECESSE EST?
SPES CERTE NEC MENS, ME REFERENTE, DEEST;
SED LEGE, ET ECCE EVEN NENTEMVE GREGEMVE TENENTEM.
PERLEGE, NEC ME RES EDERE RERE LEVES.

Eve's Legend

> Let me stress:
> the events here represented
> never reflect the trewth.
>
> Perec

Dᴇᴇᴘ ᴅᴇɴᴛᴇʟʟᴇ sᴄʀᴇᴇɴᴇᴅ, the seven green Mercedes Benzes resembled pestered sheep. They descended West End Street, swerved left, entered Temple Street then swept between the green vennels' beeches, elms 'n' elders. These trees enkernelled Exeter's See's svelte, yet nevertheless erect, steeples. Pecked men were pressed between the thermes' entrées. The screened Mercedes' secrets perplexed them:

"See them?"

"Them's yer excellence. Yer Reverend Excellence."

"Peeweet! Them's screenmen!" the set's teethless shrew yelped.

"Let's bet three pence Mel Ferrer's here!" the demented Western expert decreed.

"Excrement! Peter Sellers's the better bet!" jeered, ensemble, the TV septet.

"Mel Ferrer? Peter Sellers? Never!" yelled enreddened me. "She's Bérengère de Brémen-Brévent!"

"Bérengère de Brémen-Brévent!!" the yet reperplexed set reblethered.

"Yes! Bérengère! Bérengère 'The Qween'. Bérengère 'The Legs'. Dresden, even Leeds cheer her. The Rex, the Select, the Pleyel revere her! Bérengère, the scene's Hebe, the crème des crèmes, French fêtes', French sprees' best belle! Endless brethren cense her; when she enters the scene then sheds her dress, meteless men degender themselves!"

"Then tell me her present schemes. Peter see me? Her

63

genre, meseems, never seek vespers," the spencer-beret enshelled jerk reflected.

"Nevertheless, Bérengère's ever present chez the Reverend Excellence. He's Herbert Merelbeke's brer, see? Herbert's Thérèse Merelbeke's engenderer's engenderer; then Thérèse's Bérengère's best ephebe!"

The perplexed geezer's heben-fettered specs were deflexed, then reset:

"These brers, engenderers, ephebes seem well enmeshed!"

The jerk's senseless speech vexed me, led me where these men grew fewer, thence chez Hélène's...

Then, meseemed, the breeze between the deserted streets blew me these excerpted speeches:

"... the See effervesces..."

"... her recent endebtedness deepens..."

"... she sells her jewels..."

"Pecks?"

"... where's her fence?"

"Her fence's the Reverend Excellence's cleverness!"

"... teehee!..."

Then the breeze blew west. The rest deserted me...

Hélène dwelt chez Estelle, where New Helmstedt Street meets Regents Street, then the Belvedere. The tenement's erne-eyed keeper defended the entrée. Yet, when seven pence'd been well spent, she let me enter, serene.

Hélène greeted me, then served me Schweppes. Cheers! Refreshments were needed. When she'd devested me, she herd me eject:

"Phew! The wether!"

"Thertee-seven degrees!"

"Septembers swelter here."

She lent me her Kleenexes. They stemmed the cheeks' fervent wetness.

"Well, feel better then?"

Hélène seemed pleesed, yet reserved; expectent re the recent news. En effet. she then begged me:

"Bérengère's entered the See yet?"

"Yes."

"Perfect! Events present themselves well."

These eyes begged her tell me the deserts she expected. Free jewels?

"Heck, Bérengère's gems 'n' bezels tempt me!" she yelled.

Her extreme effervescence needed relentment, meseemed: "Yet the gems' theft'd be reckless! The See's screened. Endless tents're there, where expert peelers 'n' shrewd 'tecs dwell. We'd be demented. . ."

"We'll never be checked! We'll detect the defences' breech, then enter. The rest'll ensew."

Next, she let me redeter her, then tell her the excerpted speeches the breeze'd sent between the deserted streets: meseemed rebel men eke lechered Bérengère's jewels. We regretted the news. Hélène set her teeth. Her deep verblessness lengthened. The news'd depressed her? Never, she reneged, then sed she'd persevere, ne temere. Where led her secret, fervent reverees?

"Ernest's relentless cheek!" she yelled.

"The jerk? The self-seeker?"

"Yes, the Jerk 'n' the Seven Greek Henchmen!"

"Let's skewer them!"

"Never!" sed vehement Hélène. "The deed'd be senseless. We'd get endless pen sentences. We'd better deter them."

Her phlegm checked me. Nevertheless, her preference seemed effete.

"Ernest 'n' the henchmen's deterrent represents deep perplexedness. The weekend's here! We're stewed! We'll never enter Bérengère's den. We need the pretext."

"Feeble feller! Thérèse'll be the perfect pretext!"

"Thérèse? Thérèse Merelbeke?"

"Herself! She's deep between these sheets. The Reverend Excellence's present scheme's the weekend spent between tender wenches' sweet empressments. She's expected there!"

"Yes, Thérèse!"

Hélène's perverse yet clever scheme cheered me.

"Nevertheless, she's chez elle. Rennes's endless versts hence!"

"When'll Clément get clever? Telex her!"

The telepheme clerk preened her teeth, redressed her tresses, deterged her scent-cells then respelt the skew-lettered texts strewn between her ledgers.

"The telex pleese?"

"We're shet."

"Then when'll the telex serve me?"

"Retern efter seven."

"Yet the need's emergent!"

"The extreme emergence?"

"The emergentest extreme. 'n' these terms've been well selected."

She then let me send the telex express:

THERESE MERELBEKE. SEVEN JETEE
DES FRERES FERRET. RENNES
WE NEED, STRESS, NEED THEE.
SCHNELL! CLEMENT.

The clerk redd the telex, then entered the expense: twelve pence.

"Twelve pence! Strewth! The exces seem extreme."

"The telex never extends decrements," the severe, cheerless teller decreed.

Her twelve pence were threwn between her eyes.

Fecklessness led me hence between the Elster's scented evergreens, the fennel, the feverfew. There, meek mereless men weeled the fresh creek. They netted tench, kelt, flecked perch. Herb Bennet vended green beens, fermented crèpes; the Chester cheese ment the geezer's feet reeked. Deshevelled, vehement Celts crew the rebec's re, the crwth's te. Between the shettered chrèches stressed engenderers fed wee hens Nestlé teets. Ewes wheepled. Wrens peppered the resplendent elm trees. Bees, then fleet sphenxes swerved between the elders. Tedesche shepherds smelt red setters' ends. The steps drew me between the steep steles where we remember the Stefenssens (Zen sect members, yet even then Eyefell & Perret's welders), when they smelted the twentee-seven steel fletch cercles the Greek, then Mede sect members decreed.

The scene's sweetness sent me! Ellesmere, the elden demesne, seemed present there! The creeks. The scree. The petrels. The tempests. Then melt there! Be free! Where the ether reflects celeste resplendence, the bens' green crests, the September hemp seeds! The demesne set between the mere, then the new Tempe's cwm. Clément Theleme: there we'd resee Sceve, Sterne, Mersenne, Wegener! . . .

Tlemcen, September the seventh, MCMXXXVJJ, Mme Merelbeke engendered Thérèse. Her begetters were French. The Père, René, served between Gen. Leclerc's men. He, the tested regent, defended the dey's, then the bey's sceptres when Berber rebels pretended they were free. These events'

67

effects were: Thérèse'd been kept chez her begetters' begetters: Herbert Merelbeke, Exeter's Reverend Excellence Serge's brer; & Pernelle Merelbeke, nee Bescherelle. Herbert shepherded sheep. The herd fed the wee wenches 'n' men. Ewes' blether blessed Thérèse's sweet sleep.

Yet, René Merelbeke detested the rebels. He sed he'd skewer them. Leclerc, the serene regent, grew nettled. He felt René's schemes were extreme: be severe, yet reserved, he decreed. René seethed. He clept Leclerc "The Berbers' Bender". These vexed men then went berserk. René belted Leclerc; Leclerc beweltered then felled René.

The French HQ herd Leclerc's messengers retell these events. They expelled René. He left the French reserves then selected the Metz express. Nevertheless, Mehmet Ben Berek (he led the Berber rebels) fettered Thérèse, enjeeped her, then kept her tethered between the desert tents. Next, René's tether ended. He re-emerged between the French reserves.

"Seek the rebels!" he begged Leclerc.

"Never, Thérèse's dedd. Ben Berek slew her," Leclerc pretended.

René deserted then rented seventeen fez-dressed henchmen. Between the jebels, the deserts, the ergs where the steppes' breezes seeded then deleted defenceless weeds, here erred these henchmen, needleless brens, spent stens, nerveless épées, depleted steeds, kneeless gee-gees, bereft jennets, Thérèse's feckless seekers. Then Mehmet Ben Berek's Berbers penned themselves between the secret crests. The desert steppes were mere creekless versts, endless extents: Kef, Meknes, Zemzem, Yemen. René sensed he grew demented when he'd see these wenchless henchmen seek ewes then eschew Thérèse.

Then December ended. They were neer Memzem-

Berchem, the ex-Nemeén centre. There, René led the men between the Berbers' entrenchments. He yelled:

"Mehmet! Set Thérèse free then cede!"

"Berbers never cede! They defend the men they esteem!"

Then the rebels wrestled the rented henchmen. The sleek Berbers enmeshed René's men. Nevertheless, he lept between the tents, where heedless wenches fled pell-mell. René resembled the western tempest. He rent the tent's tegmen then Thérèse emerged, pent between Mehmet's sere enclenchment.

"Thérèse!"

"Begetter!"

"Recede René," leered Mehmet Ben Berek, the Berber's creese pressed between Thérèse's temples. "Flee hence! Lest the sweet wench gets skewered!"

"Wretch," heckled René. "Sheep's excrement! Leper's feces! Geese crèpe! Serpents' engenderment! The hempen serf the desert ferret breeds!"

"Ssssh, nerd. Respect the Berber's begetters!"

"Let the rebels fell thee! Let Ceres, let clement Hebe be present! Hell expects thee!"

Then Thérèse entervened:

"Let Merek be! Never bleed the Berber! Never revenge me! Repent! Let the peece the wenches deseyere retern between these deer tents! The best men shew clemence!"

"Eh? Eh? Thérèse? The rebel Berber's fevered her begetter's sweetest dell!?"

"Yes! Yes! He eke fevers me! Fervent, fervent fever!" Thérèse stemmered. "The fervent fever's been felt sense ferst he fettered me!"

The French kernel felt week, then yelped:

"Never! Never! Me leedle gerl!"

"Leedle gerl?" sneered the ensembled rebels 'n' hench-men. "Screw me! She's the perfect leg-between gentlemen prefer!"

"Her svelteness!"

"Her pert chest!"

"Her endless legs!"

"Her freckled cheeks!"

"Her peerless teeth!"

"Her slender neck!"

"Her tender end!"

"Her jeepers-creepers peepers!"

"Her heben tresses the breezes deshevel!"

"Be deperplexed, René Merelbeke!" Mehmet Ben Berek decreed. "Cede me Thérèse! Then sheethe the épées, the stens 'n' the brens. Let sweet peece settle between the French 'n' the Berbers. Let the desert temptresses serve thee sweet desserts between these tented settees. Then let's fête the event. Thérèse'll wed me!"

When the speech ended, Thérèse fell fervent between Meh-met's enclenchment; then René Merelbeke let them get wed.

Yet, these Berber feeders' wedded sweetees' exeestences're never eezee-peezee. Yes, there were excellent elements; yet they were breef. En effet, Mehmet's rebel sweeps perservered. Leclerc fetched René Merelbeke. Well perplexed, yet stern, he defended the Berber:

"He's Thérèse's feller! Her wedded better-self! Let's let them be!"

Nettled, Leclerc re-expelled René then reflected where best he'd repel the well-mettled Mehmet Ben Berek, lest the rebels' relentlessness ended the French presence. The Czechs, the Swedes, the Engles, the Serbs, the Medes, the Tedesche 'n' the Greeks respected the French: the presence preserved peece settlements between Brest 'n' Temenressett – they let deelers peddle free-wheel.

Leclerc, nevertheless, rejected heedlessness. He delved deep:

"Eject Mehmet? Wrestle the rebels between these jebels then skewer them? Yet we'd never be serene then, never! These Berbers resemble sleek serpents. We'll never net them. The desert dwellers defend them. The deepest secrets en-shell them. Whenever we seek them, we're checked! We'd best wheedle them, then. Detect the pretext where they'll detest Ben Berek! Teehee! Let tempests rend them! The Ber-bers' reverence's deep, yet when they've rejected the berk, he'll be stewed! The men'll seek revenge! Yes! Yes! Yet where'll we seek the pretext? Let me see… Let me see… Yep! Here's the best bet: we'll pretend the respected leeder's deep between French sheets, where he betreys the rebels' secrets! Thérèse Merelbeke'll be the perfect pretext: we'll tell them she gets her dresses chez Hermès, where she spends endless, endless checks! When Mehmet Ben Berek tells them he yet defends the Berbers, the check-tellers between here 'n' Berne, Geneve, Leeds, Dresden, Brème, even Metz'll then decree the reverse: they'll sey he sells the Berbers' demesnes, the petrel, benzene etc; then De Wendel 'n' Lesseps'll send pelf, shekels, yen! Hell, here's sense! Perverse, maybe, yet perfect!"

These, then, were the perverse – perverse's the werd – yet shrewd schemes Leclerc deveyesed. Nevertheless, when Meh-met Ben Berek yet kept the Berbers' esteem, he seemed Hell-bent: the French were neerlee defeeted. Then, when seven feys encercled her, Thérèse Merelbeke-Ben Berek resembled the Desert Qween: the deserts were chez elle; the Berbers her serfs. When she felt herself freeze, seventeen men bernt her endless trees (remember, the jebels weren't beechen green!). When her flesh seethed, her serfs blew her breezes. When she needed sleet, they'd fetch her fresh névé! Her tents were French dentelle, her bergères were cedern, her settles heben, Sèvres ewers repleted her chests!

Enwee, nevertheless, beset her. The tele'd been her pet (she'd preferred Penn's, even Stevens's westerns; yet Welles, then René Clément'd pleesed her when need be). Yet Mehmet'd never get her her set. Then, she regretted she'd ever left her French demesnes, where sedges sheltered the Scène's sleek streems, Vendée's elms, the shepherd's needle, the cresses, Denfert, even Les Ternes.

Seqwestered between the tents, she resembled Egbert Rex's qween, even Helen Keller. Her teeth were clenched. She rested speechless. She selected texts, then her meek eyes redd them: she resembled Greek-versed, Hellene-tempted clerks. The texts cheered her, they ended the spleen she felt beset her. These belles-lettres entered her tent pell-mell: Keller's 'Seven Legends', Terence, Derème, Green 'n' Greene, Genet's 'Les Nègres', Engels, Lefebvre, then Weber; Spengler then Scheeler; René Crevel then Prévert (ed. Seghers); Beckett, Verne, De Retz, then Beyle, her preference.

Yet, even then, Leclerc's schemes persevered. Weeks went beye. September left the jebels, then the telepheme clerks entered the rebel entrenchments. They left the Hermès dresses. Thérèse – the peerless *femme* – felt she'd best test them pdq.

"Perfect! These weeds pleese me! The select spencer! The dress! The tweed revers! The dentelle! Phew! These crèpe heddresses! They're excellent!"

Mehmet nevertheless never sensed the pretext, hence the rebel leeder's end. The French HQ sent there expert, Berber-dressed messengers. They entered Tlemcen, Meknès then,

between the tents, between the entrenchments, they spred
the news: well, maybe. . . yes, yes. . . hmmm, hmmm. . .

"Well, Hermès dresses're the best. . ."

"They're well deer. . ."

"Dedd deer. . ."

"Dedd deer's extreme. . ."

"Then Mehmet Ben Berek, the well-respected, meets
these expenses. . . ?"

"Else, she's been left them. . ."

"Else, they're embezzlements. . ."

"Embezzlements . . . embezzlements. . ."

Next, when these Tlemcen smeers'd been well repeeted,
the messengers'd sey:

"Meseems Mercedes 'n' Bentleys tempt Ben Berek."

Then, the exegete'd decree:

"Yep, Mehmet Ben Berek, the Berbers' well-respected
leeder's wedded French flesh. Then René Merelbeke, her begetter, serves the French presence. Yet Mehmet Ben Berek's
nevertheless the Berbers' well-respected leeder!"

These perverse exegeses entered the rebels' tents. Next,
the shrewd messengers sent them these clever leeflets:

Where're the BERBERS' needs?
The BERBERS need the deserts.
Where're DE WENDEL & LESSEPS's needs?
DE WENDEL & LESSEPS seek the deserts.
Yes, they seek the deserts' benzene.
The BERBERS respect MEHMET BEN BEREK.
MEHMET BEN BEREK seeks shekels.
Remember, THERESE dresses chez HERMES, then
remember HERMES's dresses' extreme expense!
MEHMET BEN BEREK'd never fleece the BERBER
brethren's shekels.

73

Then MEHMET BEN BEREK seeks DE WENDEL & LESSEPS's shekels!
Let the BERBER BRETHREN defend themselves!

When Mehmet Ben Berek read these smeers, he sneered:
"Let the ferrets yelp, the gerbels breed!"
Yet the Berbers' deemsters fetched Mehmet. They pestered the leeder. Thérèse's expenses lent these letters credence!
Vehement Mehmet then reneged:
"These Hermès dresses were presents the French send when they remember berths!"
Well, yes, September'd been Thérèse's berthdey.
He spent weeks there, penned between empesterments. Then he fled, re-entered the entrenchments.
Nevertheless, the secret cercle's schemes persevered. They deemed Mehmet exempt; the leeflets mere smeers. He seemed ever the Berber rebels' best brer: he'd never cede ere he'd been skewered. Yet – the yet's the essence – these smeers prevented the rebels' retrenchment. They were severe decrements. The leeders deemed they needed these events stemmed. Endeed, the rebels felt dejected. The precedent elements'd cleft the ensemblement they'd meshed.
"When the news spreds, the Berbers' ever-present needs'll be rejected!"
"We'll end degendered, senescent!"
"Endless semesters' perseverance, shelved!"
"When'll we see these events end?"
"When Mehmet's ended!"

December the seventh, when even fell, seven henchmen, the flesh's hew deeper then heben, entered the tents then slew Mehmet Ben Berek, the esteemed, well-respected rebel leeder!
Here ended Mehmet's breef reyn.

Yet the henchmen let Thérèse Merelbeke be. Her Berber ex-brethren hence detested her.

She drenched endless Kleenexes, then re-emerged chez elle.

Thérèse Merelbeke, the ex Mrs Ben Berek, then derveyeded her expert temptress's empressements between Hervé Pléven-Pleyel, Nevers's prefect, 'n' Kléber le Helder. Le Helder held her pelf. He, the fervent resercher'd breveted endless emblements. E.g.:

– the CRESCENCE-METRE, when glewed between the WC's screens, the metre lets begetters check there beybes' length;

– the SHELL-NETTER, the beechkember's best bet;

– the FLEE-FLEER;

– the GREEN-CLEERER, weeds green lees' beds, embenkments, etc;

– the NERVE-TESTER (Weber's then Fechner's reserches perfected the scheme), lets the tester see whether teeth've been well preserved;

– the SPECTRE-SEEKER, sets free steel verges when elves, weremen, revenents, etc enter the seeker's sensers;

– the BREEKS-PRESS;

– the GLEED-QWENCHER (Jenner-Seltz's BREN-METRE), when set between TNT reserves, prevents senseless events (they were freqwent ere then!);

– the SELF-FEEDER, Kléber le Helder represented the scheme hence: heben keys're wedged between seven fretted reglets; the keys' fethered crests erect themselves, swell, then eject teypers; these then seel the screens' de-centred wedges; they next set free the cemented feeder-teets; seventeen Melsen steel segments 'n' Scheffer's emergence-elements then settle the ensembled feeder. Lets begetters (even when they're exerted) feed feeble wee beybes: the rennet keeps fresh whenever the steel segments' cells remeyne clenched; when the begetters retern, they releese the cells' esse-bends, the rennet's pressed, the beybe enters then feeds, serene;

– SPENCER'S TELEMETRE, lets testers detect detrementel benzene elements, then defend themselves;

– Werner Krefeld's FEEL-THE-CREEPS, lets experts breed endless emmets, tse-tses, etc. They mey hence renege Mendel's well-esteemed Decrees;

– Etc... etc...

Rennes's telepheme clerk peered between the streets, then detected Seven, Jetée des Frères Ferret. He entered the keeper's cell:

"Mlle Thérèse Merelbeke?"

"Chest there," the keeper jested.

The clerk neered the entrée, then belled:

"Treeng! Treeng!"

"Entrez!"

He entered, tendered her the telex, extended the beret, receeved Thérèse's tenner, then left.

Thérèse resettled herself neer Kléber, then redd the telex.

"Where's the news, sweetness?" Kléber reqwested. "Tell me, these Ems Telexes pester thee?"

"The letter's Clément's. Hélène's Exeter wey. She needs me."

"When?"

"The weekend!"

"Screw me, sweetee," Kléber blethered. "Yer needs'll leeve me rejected!"

"Never fret. When we've settled Hélène's scheme, she'll resend me here. Ere then, let the reserches persevere."

"The Qenelle-Erecter depresses me. The tender we smelted never wedges them well. They tremble, then bend! The bleeders!"

Thérèse preened her heben tresses, then dressed. Kléber hem-hemmed three Meyerbeer verses then entered the velvet breeches he prefered.

Between the French then Exeter beeches, the jet cleft the ether. Tee qwenched Thérèse's therst; the *Express* held her eyes:

"Eestern Dépêche: Brejnev'll see the Medes when September's ended."

"Messmer's secret schemes."

"Belem'd seen Che's end, J. F. Revel reveels."

"Mendès's Célèbes Letter."

"Servent-Scheber: they'll meet ere seventee-seven!"

"The *Express*'s Deep Enqwest: Shell-Berre reneges re benzene's extreme expense."

"Letters: The Keep-Well Secret? Semple! Chew greens!"

"Between Sens & Nevers, Mercx led even when he'd rent seven nerve centres!"

"*Eden, Eden, Eden*: September's best seller?"

"Denver's Meegeren's Vermeer's?"

Hélène reqwested gen:

"Where's the Rennes jet, pleese?"

"Next, then left!" yelled the desk clerk.

The jets resembled fleet sledges when they speed between the steppes. The Rennes jet descended, then entered Exeter's demesnes. Men left the jet, then wedged themselves between the exets. Hélène peeked, peered, yet never detected Thérèse.

"Hélène!" screeched Thérèse. She'd seen her between the desks, then yelled.

"Thérèse!"

The tender wenches pecked cheeks.

"Yer the bee's knees!"

"Reelee?"

"'n' well-dressed! These fennec pelts're well neet!"

"Mehmet left me them. Nevertheless, yer'll get lent them!"

"Yer the best!"

"Where's Clément?"

"He's chez Estelle. Let's get fed ferst."

"Yes, let's."

They went chez "Mme Berthe's", Exeter's selectest crème's preferred eeteree. The meels there were endeed excellent. Reysed neer Besse-en-Chendesse, her French chef'd served chez René, neer Les Ternes. He'd been the best chefs' treynee: the Père blenc (Belley-en-Bresse), the Frères Vernet, de Mende, Bébert Lévèqe, de Clèves, etc, etc.

They entered. Mme Berthe led them between the credences, neer where the street screens were. The servers resettled the dessert shelves' dentelles, then set the Sèvres ewers 'n' trenchers.

Mme Berthe herself tended the wenches, helped them get settled, secreted Thérèse's tress-net, then Hélène's tweed beret, then begged them select between these excellent refreshments:

ENTREES

Bettered Whelks

Wren Freeters

Peesweet's Eggs

Eels en Gelée

Kedgeree

The Frère Vernet's Béchémelles

Geese Leevers en Crêpe
Smeeched Skegger

ENTREMETS
Breyzed Perch
Tench flesh strewn between cress
Deer's Selles
Leveret nestled between betel kernels
Peppered Bell-Wether
Vendéen Grebes
Hen's legs en merrette
Jerked beef served between French herbs
Wennerschnetzel

THE VEG
Vermeecelles
French Been Qenelles
Fresh Green Beens, Swedes, Fennel, Pees, Ers, Vetch

THE CHEESE CREDENCE
Fermented Rennet
Chester
Treble Lester

Bretzels

DESSERTS
Sweet Sherbert
Peech Belle-Hélène
Xerex Treyefle
Blermenge
Reversed Creem
Werner Pretzels
Crêpes Flembés
Mme Berthe's Tendernesses

79

Thérèse sed she'd never eeten Mme Berthe's tenderness.

"They're crêpe dentelles, qwetsch, then Crème de Menthe!"

"Mmmmmm! Let's get them!"

"St Estephe? Gevrey? Vergelesse? The Vergelesse's excellent. . ."

Nevertheless, Thérèse preferred the St Estephe.

They served themselves, then chewed the beef. The segments resembled nerve-ends. Vexed, they reprehended Mme Berthe:

"The beef's mere repellent lether!" Hélène yelled.

"Then there's the detergent stench!" Thérèse screeched.

Mme Berthe went green, then fetched the chef. He entered, reddened, then stemmered:

"We regret. . . never precedent. . . we'll renew. . ."

"See where he trembles, the twerp!" Thérèse jeered.

They left the rest, threw the perks between the trenchers, then left.

Even then, Bérengère de Brémen-Brévent left her Mercedes.

She'd eke selected Mme Berthe's.

The wenches met between the exets.

"Bérengère! Well met!"

"Thérèse! Perfect!"

They expressed endless tendernesses. Then Bérengère begged her news.

"Well, the weekend's here. Hélène 'n' Estelle've reqwested me Exeter wey."

"Hélène? Estelle? Never met them."

"They're the best temptresses we've ever met."

Thérèse then presented Hélène. Hélène 'n' Bérengère pecked cheeks.

"Pleesed. . ."

"Reelee. . ."

Thérèse then begged her tell whether she slept chez the perverse, yet Reverend Excellence.

"Yes! The weekend sees the Excellence well-fettled. The clerks expect sweet empressements!"

"Teehee! The lewdest fête's sweetest pretext!"

Then the wenches leered between themselves. They resembled ewes when sweet herbs've fed them.

"Few wenches, yet endless vergers!"

"Phew!"

"Strength, the revels we'll get!"

"We'll expect thee, then. 'N' sweet Hélène?"

"Yes, yes, even Estelle. . ."

The precedent events' présee:

Bérengère de Brémen-Brévent (B de BB, men hecht her BB) deems she needs her jewels vended. Exeter's Reverend Excellence, Serge Merelbeke'll be her fence. Yet the lewd lecher never schemes except when he'll get sex, revels, sweet empressements, etc.

Hélène reckens the gems'll be hers. She enters Exeter, then dwells chez Estelle 'n' Clément (me, remember), Estelle's brer, then Hélène's temp. geezer.

Thérèse Merelbeke (her engenderer's begetter's the Reverend Excellence's brer) gets telexed. She's Bérengère's best ephebe, yet Hélène needs her help.

Even then, Bérengère's jewels tempt Ernest the Messer 'n' the Seven Greek Henchmen.

When she leeves Mme Berthe's, Thérèse meets Bérengère. Hélène'd expected the meet. She gets herself presented. Her scheme's dedd elementree: peelers 'n' 'tecs ensweep the well-defended See, yet Bérengère's begged her presence there between the Reverend Excellence's revels.

Then, when Hélène's entered the See, B de BB's necklesses 'n' bezels'll be eezee meet. . .

Get me?

Nevertheless, even then, Ernest the Messer meddled. He'd never resemble Fernendel, trew, yet here he represented deep perplexedness.

Between the Seven Greek Henchmen, he entered "Bert's", Exeter's best theeves' preferred den. Eleven yeggs heckled then encercled them. When Ernest'd belted severel hedds, the feyeghts ended. Then, when the yeggs'd left, Bert redressed the benches then let them reqwest refreshments: Fred the Ted preferred tee; Jesse Jeymes crème de menthe; the Benedek Brethren (Seth 'n' Stephen) xerex; Peter Pence ESB; Bellfree Bebel the seyme. Then Ernest? Lewd-End Lew? They hemmed the wheyele then selected Schweppes.

Bert served them; then the vessels qwenched the men's therst.

They fell speechless.

"We're never pressed yet. Nevertheless. . ." Ernest decreed.

"Yes, yes, cheef," yessed the Seven Henchmen.

"Yer redeemless bleeders. . ."

"Eh cheef?" The henchmen defended themselves. "The wether swelters!"

"Well, well, where's the gen?"

"See, cheef, the news's the See's well encercled. Shet! We'll never breech the peelers' defences!"

"Defences! Defences!" yelled Ernest. "Yet the jewels're there!"

"Yep, the jewels're there. When we get there, then we'll

fleece them; yet we'll never get there, hence we're stemmed. Here we rest. Screwed!"

Next, the Seven Henchmen reblethered these cheerless vewes: when the den's well-defended, they're beet; the theft'd be mere recklessness. They'd be berserk! They'd better fleece beybe's sweetees!

Ernest's tether ended:

"Shet them, ne'er-be-wells, nerveless benders!"

The vexed henchmen's teeth were set.

"Yer blessed the cheef sees where he sees!" he yelled.

Then he sed he'd seen Bérengère enter Mme Berthe's, even when Thérèse 'n' Hélène emerged.

The event's sense never entered the henchmen's hedds.

"?!?"

"Senseless nerds! Hélène!"

"Hélène?"

"Clewless Theses! Hélène de Mehler-Werfel!"

"Hélène de Mehler-Werfel? The eezee ley?"

"The sex-peddler!"

"The cheep screw!"

"The rest's dedd cleer," went Ernest's exegeses: "Hélène seeks B de BB's gems; Thérèse's her helper; she's the Reverend Excellence's neece; Thérèse enters the See, then presents Hélène!"

Dessembled between Bert's gents, the screens let me here these secret speeches. The seventh sense! The nerve! Ernest's nerve, leyekweyese. He seemed the theeves' Hegel. Endeed, he'd been well edjewkeyted when he'd spent the thertee yeres' pen sentence. He'd redd Berkeley, René Le Senne, Herbert Spencer etc!

Then the steel nerves led me between the henchmen.

"Strewth!" jeered Ernest. "We tell the men the gen re the wenches, then the gents eject the geezer!"

The bench they'd left free settled me, serene.

"Hets! They're repellent!" the ephebes yelled.

"Get screwed, benders!" they herd me repleye.

"Let yer sex preferences be," Ernest decreed. "Clément's entered the den. Hence, meseems, he seeks help."

"Clever wee Ernest. Yet the term 'help' seems extreme. Let's be cleer: we seek *entente*."

"Where we let the wenches be?"

"Yes. They respect thee. We never seek fewds."

"Hmmmm. Then where's the *entente* they seek's pretext?"

"Bérengère's gems. . ."

Ernest went red.

"We'll never let these detested wenches meddle!"

"Eezee. . . eezee. . . jest let yer henchmen enter the See, then see the peelers net them! Yer stewed!"

Then Ernest delved deep:

"Well. . . Hélène, Estelle then Clément'll enter. Bérengère 'n' the Reverend Excellence'll let them. We see the scheme! Then where'll me 'n' the henchmen be?"

"Between the See's secret exets!"

"The secret exets?"

"Yes, Thérèse's the gen. . ."

Ernest's bleed-vessels reddened the jerk's temples. He seethed.

"Yer scheme leeves me perplexed."

"Wheye?"

"The wenches let me enter, yes?"

"Yes yes."

"Then where's the deel. . ?"

"Get clever. The jewels. . ."

"Even-Stevens?"

"Thertee per cents: Thérèse thertee, Hélène thertee. . ."

"Then me thertee. . . 'n' the rest?"

"Leedle erners tempt certen men. . ."

Ernest seemed well tempted, yet begged the henchmen's experteese:

"Hey, Lew, where's the ketch?"

Lewd-End Lew then sed he'd penetreyte the schemer's secrets. The jerk's expert eyes tested me; teeth chewed me. The wren, when serpent-spelled, resembled defenceless me then.

Sleek, fremescent Lew then sneered these few sentences:

"The geezer's bent. He'll peddle the peelers the pelf."

"Well, Clément?" Ernest begged me.

"Well. . . Well. . ."

"Where's yer defence?"

These events needed reel street cred, meseemed. The merest feebleness, then the henchmen'd skewer me! Let's steel the vertebrers, then send the p 'n' m tender ferewells! Then Lethe sent me her dreems: remember, when we were green between the ferns, the ferst rennet teeth, the wee tresses' rebel emblements, the heedlessness, the sprees! The crèpe-seeled feet! The medderleynes we'd drench whenever we'd serve tee! The ten beye ten metres sped between the elder-strewn sedges! December's endless freeze, then when the névé'd melted we'd see Vendée's sweet shepherdesses! Then *Phèdre, Esther,* the Pleyel *Belle Hélène* we'd seen! Even Bébert de Flers! The eleven+, Greek, the belles-lettres! Heck, were ever these theses presented: Terence's, Sceve's metres, the feet, the enjembements, the epentheses?!

"Hey, geezer, there yet?" Ernest reqwested.

These gentle reverees then left me. Mey the Endless Begetter be clement! Never let me enter Hell!

"Lew's werds were mere nether breezes! Hélène sent me.

Beleeve her, else reject her. Then get screwed. Eyether wey, Clément's exempt."

"Hey, cheef, let's get the bleeder!" yelled Fred the Ted.

Meseemed the Beretters were set. Me nether cheeks clenched.

"Keep serene, Fred. Let me reflect," Ernest decreed.

Vehement theses then wended between the jerk's fevered nerve-ends. He rested there perplexed, fell-tempered. Yet the defences seemed weekened. They begged me retempt the nerd:

"Where's the ketch?" he herd me serggest. "The therd sleyece's best when men need bred!"

Even these terms never cleered Ernest's vewes. Yet he tested them, weyed them. Where ley the breech? The henchmen's perfect speechlessness let needles be herd where they fell.

"Where's the ketch?" he herd me repeet.

Fell Lewd-End Lew sqweezed herpes-flecked cheeks, then shewed me the few teeth he'd left. Meseemed they sed: "We see threw yew, geezer, we'll get yew, never fret!" Bellfree Bebel reddened the next Kent; Peter Pence bezzled ESB.

Lengthened seyelent spells went beye. They seemed weeks, semesters even, then Ernest sed these breef, yet cleer sentences:

"Well," the serpreme leeder decreed, "let's beleeve Hélène..."

Stephen Benedek left the bench, then rebelled:

"Jest let me sey..."

Stern Ernest entervened:

"Never! Never! We're the deemster, 'n' we've deemed, get me? Whenever the men welsh, we'll redress them! Redefect, 'n' we'll see thee penned!"

Stephen Benedek went green, then resettled. Ernest left the bench. He decreed the meet's end:

"Well men, let's get fed. Schnell, there, schnell!"

The henchmen erected themselves. Fred the Ted entered the gents. Jesse Jeymes's tresses were repreened. They herd me reqwest:

"When's the next meet then?"

"Yep, when?" went Ernest.

"The eventheyeme?"

"Ten efter seven."

"Perfect. Where?"

Ernest's scent-cells flexed whenever he reflected:

"Needle Street."

"Needle Street?"

Ernest's berth never fell yestereve, beleeve me! The Needle Street meet sent me the creeps.

"The wenches detest Needle Street then?"

"Never! They even prefer the Needle Street scene. We'll be there."

Then we left.

Needle Street, Exeter's hep set's den, ley neer the See, between Ethelbert Crescent 'n' Temple Street. The street's excesses were centred where the few breeze-swept elms encercled Werner Ebersweld's resplendent green-pebbled "Keetchener's Steed". Here, desprette dregs slept between the benches; when newer nepenthes (beer, reefers, ether, L S D, speed, etc) sent them frenzeed, they resembled Verlène's legenderee "Green Feys". Fleet Eden's endless qwest held these helpless sleepers enserfed: there were Medes, Greeks, deserted Sergents, hennered Germen, Khmers, dredd-tressed Negresses, the Gretchen 'n' her kneeless yet emblemed genes, tee-pee dwellers, deshevelled geezers when they'd left Memel, Denver, Esterel's crests 'n' the demesnes the Tennessee drenches, well-phlegmed wenches, the beet-set the Beetles' verses sent fervent.

The breezes reeked there, where teethless deelers peddled ether. There, the hempen wretches resembled mere beests. They herded between the WCs where herb experts delt them hexed reefers.

There, crewless twerps, sheyved Zen-sect members (hedds leyeke sleek eggs) peeled feeble bells then begged pence. Here, the depleted wench'd preen her flees; there, she'd let her leper-flecked nether end's germs breethe free. These demented dregs resembled dedd, erth-cemented trees. Herbless dedd-beets left wretched tenements then crept, then schlept where they'd get the reefers they needed: deth's hedds, yestereve's beer lees, the skelertens where De Qweencee's 'n' Bewdelère's spectres yet dwelt! Mere belches the breezes blew!

Needle Street. Here, then, were the scenes Ernest preferred. Yet where ley the schemer's deepest secrets? These spent spectres' demesne, these kef-demented sects, the dreems Hell encercles repelled me, sent me between the Belvedere 'n' New Helmstedt Street, then drew me chez Estelle.

She served me tee, wheyele Hélène 'n' Thérèse dressed.

"Let's get! Schnell!" she herd me decree when the settee'd settled me.

"Ernest's set?" she begged me, then served ferther refreshments.

"Set then netted! Phew, let me tell ewe, Lewd-End Lew'd preferred me skewered. We're blessed Ernest's dense!"

Next, resplendent Thérèse, then belle Hélène entered the den.

They herd me retell the precedent events, then reveel the meet Ernest'd reqwested.

"Needle Street?" Thérèse repeeted. "Where's the bleeder's scheme?"

"He'll get the hemp, meybe!" Estelle jested.

"The hemp seed's never tempted Ernest!" we reneged.

"Well stew me!" Hélène yelped. "The bleeder's scheme's creestel! Where's Werner Behrens's beet? Needle Street!"

"The terd!"

"Exeter's werst! The Spengler-fervent ex-Feldwebel even yet regrets Bergen-Belsen's end!"

"Ernest expects the news'll freyeghten me. Never! Screw Behrens!" Hélène screeched.

Her werds weren't reelee trew. She went green, seemed dejected. Her eyes begged me help.

"Let me get the creep! He'll get sqweezed between these feelers then ejected between the SS brethren!"

"Never let them get thee!" the wenches blethered tergether.

"Sweetees, Clément's end'll be yeers hence, beleeve me!"

Then the tender wenches pecked me ferewell. Between the stens, we selected the Beretter Pepe'd left me (we then remembered the geezer's deeds 'n' the excellent exemple he'd left), then the Lewger (Peter Cheney's present). Next, Exeter's streets led me where we yessed Behrens the werst'd be.

Exeter's endless; theeves' dens teem there. Bert's screens were shettered; Needle Street's metres were then retrekked, yet Behrens's den'd be elsewhere, meseemed. Needle Street ernt Behrens's gelt – there he delt reefers, rented tenements, lent seven pence then re-embezzled twelve, these perfect leedle erners he'd never declere – yet the world's Behrenses prefer des. reses. where Gettees, Debs, French Grendees, the relm's peers, etc dwell. They're gentlemen's gentlemen. They've the best fernetcher: Chesterfeeld settees, heben credences, Regencee desks 'n' the rest! When they feed belle-lettreests, penmen, exegetes, sketchers, etchers, etc they even pretend they're Meyeceeneses!

The veyn qwest led me between the dens, the shebeens, the keyfs, the beer cellers: "The Select", "Ye Three Brewers", "The Green Messenger", "Chez Derek", "The Seven Elves", "Herbert's Shelter", "The Essex", "The Bell Wether", "The French Letter", where beermen served me seltzers then sed they'd never seen the Feldwebel.

Well, the news depressed me. Then the seventh sense remembered the bleeder Behrens freqwented Edmée d'Erme de Beetch, the French meydeme, the setter-between!

Jeez, Edmée repelled me! She fleeced wee wenches, even fledgelets, then left them between perverted gentlemen's feelers. These sweet defenceless deers (they resembled new-weened ewes) then served the gentlemen's lewd preferences. These excesses ment freqwent meyhem. Demented, dejected begetters'd netted sevrel gentlemen then skewered them. The peelers'd then seqwestered them. Next, the begetters' defence breefs entered the pen. They begged the Prefect delve deep, detect the trewth, then decree severe sentences. The Prefect pledged he'd help. Yet the perverted gentlemen were the Prefect's frends! He never erected except between wee wenches' nether cheeks! The peelers' reserches were checked; they preferred r 'n' r, hence they repressed the rewmers then qwenched the press. Meenwheyele, Edmée knew she'd never be sentenced, hence her fell efferes persevered!

There 'n' then, Edmée d'Erme de Beetch's den drew me. She dwelt neer the Elster, where Kernell Street meets Needle Street.

The street's bleekness secreted me, then her peech-trees helped me enter her defences. The street level seemed emptee, yet the next level's sheen reveeled her presence. Then where were the needed steps? Screw me! The sewer-feeder let me, well exerted, reech the ferst ledge where, the spell seemed weeks, the screens' defences were breeched, then the den descreetlee entered. Yet where were the creeps? The pleyce seemed deserted.

Well, gentle reeders, even then the seventh sense let me detect them: Ernest, Behrens, Fred the Ted 'n' Edmée, where these celebreyted sweyene preyed breedge!

"Seven herts!"

"The grend slem!!"

"Therteen treecks!!!"

"The sqweeze!!!!"

"Cheyeld's pley. Eezee peezee! We'll eject the qween, then Fred'll leed, he'll sqweeze Edmée's ten, then the rest's set!"

They never herd me set the Lewger. The screens wrecked, Fred, the Feldwebel then Edmée were peppered streght sets!

Ernest the messer reeled then went green. He trembled. He resembled mere greengeyge gelée. The serch he let me meyke reveeled the steel shells the bleeder's trews dessembled. Ernest revered these deddlee shells whenever he'd wreek the revenge sleek serpents prefer.

"Eh?" he mermered. "Me next, eh?"

"Dedd Ernest's dedd ernest," he herd me jest.

The wey deer Ernest's trembles persevered meyde me feel sleyetlee tender: "Settle there."

He heeded the reqwest, then the few hemp metres they'd left there let me tether the berk. He resembled mermeefeyed Egeepshens.

Then Fred's, Behrens's 'n' Edmée's seets were re-erected.

Edmée's settled me. Then, the Kents detected, Ernest herd me sey:

"Let's rest. Here, smeech?"

Ernest's clenched teeth receeved the Kent. Yet, members leyeke steel, vertebrers streyghtened, he seemed neer demented. Let the jerk stew there, then. The den needed extended reserches.

Jeez! Edmée d'Erme de Beetch reckened herself the bees' knees! The reel cheese! Weren't her dens dedd neet!? She led Reyeley's leyefe chez elle. Even the WCs were resplendent! Then the bedrewms! The derns were trew extremes! Dentelle, velvet, rep 'n' seelk kertens! The bed'd nestle seventeen wenches between the sheets! Then the peekchers! Vermeer de Delft screens, Klee pen 'n' eenks, Ernst sketches! Then Eschers, Légers, Getzlers, Debrés, Estèves (even Vertèses)! Them wee wenches'd been well peddled!

The telepheme detected, the wenches were genned:

"Belvedere ten seven three?"

"Yes?"

"Hélène?"

"Yes."

"Clément here. The geese're stewed. Yer expected chez the ex Mme Edmée!"

"Kernell Street?"

"Kernell Street."

There 'n' then, Ernest herd me retern. He seemed better. Repepped. Refreshed even.

"Where'd Clément, the wretched get, get the nerve? Merder the henchmen! When we held thee, chez Bert, we'd've skewered thee, never swett. Yet we preferred the *entente*. Nevertheless, the rest'll defend themselves. We'll get revenge!"

"Heed me, geezer. Leeve yer heyegh steed, then see sense! The *entente* we settled sed the henchmen'd help Hélène.

92

She'll let them enter the See, they help themselves, then fleece B de BB's gems!"

"Yep!"

"Then get me! We're shrewd. We see yer schemes! Hence the Feldwebel 'n' the French meydeme get ledded. See? When they're the reserves, where's the ferepley?"

Ernest's tense teeth then ejected:

"Dreck! The Prefect defends Edmée! The peelers'll get thee, else the henchmen. Yer screwed, geezer."

Hell, he nettled me! The jerk's teeth receeved three belts. The bleeder, well bled, fell speechless.

"See sense, Ernest. Never heckle me."

The teeth he'd left reddened ten kleenexes. He let me stem the streem. Meseemed we'd better resettle the *entente*.

"We regret the regretted Fred. We never schemed the deer feller's end. Nevertheless, were he yet here, he'd've felled me!"

"Yer felled enywey!" Ernest repeeted.

"Let yer teeth rest when we cleen them! Remember, the leeder's ME! The next jerk we see welsh'll resemble Fred, get me?"

"Yep, yer the leeder here. Yet, beleeve me, Ernest'd never enter yer shewes!"

"Never recken yew'll berree me!"

When Ernest seemed serener, we detethered the nerd then resecreted the Lewger.

"Senseeble Ernest, perfect! The eventheyeme'll see me, thee, yer henchmen 'n' the wenches even-stevens: the deeds'll be the seyme, the deyngers the seyme, the effects the seyme. We fleece Bérengère's gems 'n' her necklesses, then we'll be serene. Keep together, then we keep the ergreement; defect then yer benders 'n' yew'll get felled, reyeght?"

"Reyeght. We'd better sey yes."

Then we herd feetsteps between the peech trees. Let them be the wenches'! Ernest's benders' presence'd never tempted me less. . .

When Estelle, Thérèse then Hélène entered they resembled Helen when her feyce set seyl endless treyeremes, else new Eves when serpents tempt them: the crêpe dresses were mere sketches the breezes blew, then reveeled theyeghs 'n' nether cheeks. Ernest seemed speechless:

"Phew! They're reet perteete, yer wenches!"

Estelle 'n' Thérèse seemed pleesed when they herd these preyses. Yet Hélène, when she'd seen where the sleyn ley, stretched herself then decreed:

"End the speel! Let's get set!"

Then she let me tell her the recent events.

"Where're the henchmen?" she enqweyered.

"Needle Street's the meet."

Then dedd serene, phlegm-repleted, the leederene tensed herself: her fermness'd settle the fewcher events.

"Well, Clément'll enter Needle Street then fetch Ernest's men. We'll meet between the See's elm trees. Cleer?"

"Yep."

"Feyene. Meenwheyele, Estelle 'n' Ernest'll detect the See's secret entrence, then enter. The cellers'll then secrete Ernest. When he heers Clément yell, he'll re-emerge. Remember?"

"The elephent never. . ."

Hélène severed the berk's speech:

"Mey we expect wee leedle Ernest, then?"

Vexed, he fell verbless.

"Estelle'll enter the Reverend Excellence's enteecheymber, stey there, then we'll fetch her."

"Where'll the henchmen be? When'll we see them next?"

"When Clément's fetched them. . ."

"The scheme reeks," Ernest yelled.

"Hey, Ernest," we jeered, "see scents!"

"The Reverend Excellence expects me!" Hélène resewmed. "Let's hence. . . Schnell! Seek," she begged me, "three sheets then shelve these decedent wretches. . ."

Well, the See certenlee effervesced.

"We're set? We're set?" begged the Reverend Excellence. "The e'en's events'll erect me, meseems. Let the wenches enter!"

"Shell we get them, Excellence?" Reverend Spencer reqwested.

Reverend Spencer, the Ley Brer, Exeter's deen, the Excellence's dexter member, the *emeenence greeze*, served the See's needs.

"Ney, let them be, Reverend Spencer. Nevertheless, pleese precede me! We'll detect the few eyetems the dens yet need, then see whether the See'll meet the lewd reqweyerements we mey feel."

Trewlee, the See seemed endless: there were seven seycred temples. The extreme western temple'd been selected then ferneshed: the revels'd be held here. The entrence resembled the Greek nerthex, the beechen chesses were pleyned, lengthened then met the cedern pelmets where they stretched beneeth. Next were the WCs: here were severer peerced settles, set between well-hewn screens. These then led between the kweyer's smelted steel, where ley the See's western neyve. The neyve feetchered severel velvet-screened dens where revels were eke held: the preceyese den depended. The Reverend Excellence's precepts were ferm: he'd let the clerks steyte there preferences re these certenlee lewd "scenes", yet, when present, he stressed they respect stern decrees. When they rebelled, they were freqwentlee expelled.

R'n'r between these excellent dens seemed well neet: the kerpets were velveteen weft, else Keyshmeer; sheep's fleeces were strewn between the settees, settles, serpent-legged bergères, creem-serge seets 'n' green-rep benches. There were even pews, where the clerks rested when the revels' mere specteckle tempted them. Set between chehndeleers, severel eemense cerges smeeched. Eveedentlee, the dens smelt encensed. Certen brethren even sed they reeked. Endeed, the Reverend Excellence revered censers – he thence remembered seycred servesses – hence he decreed the See's dens be esperged eech even.

Reverend Spencer then the Emeenence exhemened the dens. The gleefell Excellence beemed:

"Well, perfect! The spree'll be excellent!"

"Then when'll the serfs dress thee?" Reverend Spencer mermered.

Well, there 'n' then. The Reverend Excellence entered the vestree, where he'd be devested, beythed, deterged, preened, then redressed: chevrette shewes 'n' crewel shert.

Then he reflected whether he'd weyre the heben egrette's fethers. He decked them, then shed them, then redecked them. He heseeteyted. Then the clerks shewed the Excellence's refleckshen.

"Fegs!" he reflected. "Ye'd never gess we were seventee! We're well-fettled yet! See the svelteness! The chest! The legs! Eh, Reverend Spencer?"

"The Emeenence's perfectedness leeves me speechless!"

Here, the lengthened dress-scene ended. The Reverend Excellence left the vestree, then redescended the steps.

∗ ∗ ∗

Meenwheyele, between the next den's screens, Bérengère de
Brémen-Brévent leyekweyese decked, rejected, then redecked
her gems, necklesses, perls yet (here she resembled the
Emeenence) she remeyned perplexed:

"Deck them? Else secrete them?"

Yet dress-sense never entered her hedd: beseyede her
resplendence, the jewels seemed sheenless.

"There'll be endless clerks, then cheep wenches! When
the theef gets tempted, these jewels'll get fleeced!"

Then shrewd Bérengère let her cleverness werk. She felt
she'd best secrete her jewels there. Her steel chests'd shelter
them. The keys entered the breeches then freed the defences.
She next emmewed her chests between the shelves. These,
her keys then penned ferm. She ferst reckened she'd better
dessemble these keys, then, when she'd remembered the
"Fleeced Letter" precept, she left them where they were,
defenceless, neer her bedsted. Next, she descended chez the
Reverend Excellence. Even then, Thérèse 'n' Hélène entered.

"Deer, sweet wenches, well met, well met! Ye resemble
Qweens!" the Reverend Excellence beemed.

"Let me," went Thérèse, "serve the Excellence's ends!"

"Well see, well see," he repleyed. "Here's Bérengère!"

She then entered.

"Bérengère, sweetest, these hevenlee wenches' presence
here well pleeses me. When'll we settle the debt?"

"Meseems," sed the Reverend Spencer, "these wenches
represent sereneness's perfect threeness. They'll bless the
revels!"

Then he receyeted these excellent verses:

Eve, September's belle, then the Greek mermen:
Where drew these helms, where've swevens sent me?

Helen, we revered thee, perverse heben –
The Lethe where we erred, sere sexèd scree.

Where left we the seed we'd shed between ferns?
The meek sentence spelt the bens' endlessness;
Seven wenches wrestled Demeter's sweet kerns;
Then the seed we strew begets the temptress:

She lets the lees be green (the term she threw),
Seven needles press her (September's mew),
Where Eden-fettered Eve the freeze defends.
Never be speechless, never reject me –

The venter sheens red where the tempted tends:
Let these sere swevens, then September flee.

"These effete e-feet seem excellent!" the Reverend Excellence jested.

"Never reject them!" Bérengère decreed. "Be they lewd, be they perverse. Eezee feet send me fervent!"

Next, they entered the den, where the settees settled them.

"Reverend Spencer!" the Emeenence begged. "Seek the clerks then fetch them here!"

He left the settle then the den.

"Then let me fetch the ephebes we expect" Hélène reqwested.

"Benders?" yelled Bérengère. "We'll never need them!"

"Let her fetch them, deer B de BB," the Reverend Excellence decreed. "The clergee freqwentlee prefer men. We let the clerks here see them, whenever they elect."

"Nevertheless, shert-reysers..."

"Let preferences be references! Never redd Theleme's emblem?"

"Well, yes..." Bérengère ceded.

Hélène, leyeke the Reverend Spencer, then left. She fetched the teem.

Hélène returned. She preceded me, me Estelle, she Ernest, then the henchmen. There they weyted: Jesse Jeymes, Peter Pence, Bellfree Bebel, the Benedek brethren (these gemels were never seen seprette), then Lewd-End Lew.

When the Reverend Spencer'd entered between the ensembled clerks, Hélène presented her teem; then he presented the clerks:

"Tencrède de Stenbergen, he's the perverse verse expert; Edme de Bénévent, when he belts nether cheeks, they remeyn reddened fer weeks! Kenneth Peebles, the belch 'n' fell nether breezes expert; René Vernet, the fervent pecker-jerker; Herbert Scheele, he freqwentlee prefers men; wheyele Celse Delesert prefers beests; then Stephen Brewster, he's well-esteemed between the Engles' sheets!"

"Hmmm," went Bérengère. "Well-esteemed, eh? Where's the pretext?"

"Let's see," the serene Emeenence repleyed.

Stephen Brewster's breeks were descended, then the begetter's jewels he'd receeved were reveeled. Hell, the hewje member seemed elephenteene! Yet the sweetest, yes the sweetest elements were the sleek sketches he'd pleyced there. They represented perfect French, Greek, Engleesh Qweens!

"Jeez, seyve me the Qweens!" yelped Thérèse. The weerdness exceyeted her.

She knelt then drew Stephen's member between her teeth. Eveedentlee, these events neerlee set the revels en treyn. Nevertheless, the Reverend Excellence felt he'd better speek ferst, then left the pew where he'd been:

"Deer brethren! Sweet temptresses! The scenes we see here pleese me! They bespeek excellent revels! Let the encense be esperged! The Xerex, the Genevrette served! Let the peckers be erect, the clefts spred weyede! Let the fête kermence, then mey these perverse empressements pleese the Eternel Begetter!"

The speech ended, he resettled. He resembled the severest gentlemen.

"The Reverend Excellence's stern!" jested Estelle 'n' Hélène.

They then French-necked the Emeenence, were sqweezed between the lewd elder's teeth.

"Let the Excellence be jerked!" begged sweet Estelle.

"Pleese, pleese, deerest hert," went he.

Estelle reysed the needless shert, then descended the trews (they were, eveedentlee, M'n'S trews, the best) then expertlee encercled the Reverend Excellence's feeble wee feller.

"Eezee! Eezee!" he yelped. "Keep serene!"

Next, wheyele Stephen's elephenteene member swelled 'n' swelled between Thérèse's cheeks, wheyele the Reverend Excellence's pecker neered erekshen between Estelle's jerks, Bérengère entered the revels, then the Reverend Spencer, the clerks, the henchmen 'n' me.

Speechless, the clerks peered when Bérengère, the Qweenteese, shed her dress, shewed her slender legs, her cheeks' perfect spheres, then the secret temple where endless, endless men'd entered.

"Hell, she sends me!" Lewd-End Lew sqweeled. "Wenches tempt me, then? Help!"

Bellfree Bebel devested, then ley beseyede Lew:

"Bérengère never sent thee, pecker-hedd! These cheeks were the temptresses. Then get between them, pdq!"

Wheyele these tender benders embreyced, Thérèse left Stephen's member; sperm drenched her cheeks.

"Jeez, the geezer's well-pended! He's the reel sceptre! The épée!"

She shed her dress, settled between the pews, spred her legs, then the Reverend Spencer herd her yell:

"Hey, Rev! Rev me pleese!"

He devested then speeded where she ley.

"Hmmm," went she. "We've the reel wee weellee wenkee here!"

"The member mey be wee, yet we're ever reddee," he cleymed, then entered her. They screwed stederlee.

Well, the cheynge between Stephen's hewjness then Spencer's meek mete seemed cleer; yet the cheynge nevertheless cheered Thérèse:

"Strewth! The pecker's sheer steel! Hevven!"

Meenwheyele, Hélène left the Reverend Excellence 'n' Estelle; she tendered Ernest her end. He rejected her:

"Men're the best. The feeble sex's repellent!"

"Then the feeble sex seys: get screwed!" she yelled, then let her nether breezes blew.

The stench exceyeted Ernest. He fetched Peter Pence, then they held her between them:

"Depreyved shrew! Geys get thee, eh? Then get these!"

"Then we'll get these!" checked Peter.

Hélène's bleets resembled ewes' when Peter's mettled member entered her cheeks, then Ernest spred her legs 'n' penetreyted her beever.

Yet, even pent between these gemel peckers, Hélène seemed gleeless. She heyled the rest:

"Hey! The benders, here! We need the enteyere septet!"

The Benedek brethren, Bebel, Lew then Jesse Jeymes

hence encercled her. Jesse Jeymes erected three pews, then cleyembed neer her teeth. She serenlee blew the member, her feelers jerked Bebel 'n' Lew, wheyele her expert feet sent the Benedek brethren berserk!

The ephebes' exemple enspeyered the clerks: they leyekweyese encercled Thérèse. She then left the Reverend Spencer.

Next, Bérengère ley neer me, then seezed me between her stretched legs. She drew me between them, then let me strehddle her. She tweeked the pecker between her teeth, let me sqweeze her brests, chew her teets, then descend between her theyeghs.

"Yer sew wet, ewe drench me, sweetee!"

"Eet me! Eet me!" she yelped, then pressed the testes she held between her feelers.

Meenwheyele, Estelle persevered. The jerks she rendered the Reverend Excellence's pecker never ceesed, yet the expected sperm steyed pent. Endeed, the Emeenence's yeers were seventee, 'n' elders' members're verveless, nerveless, dreeree.

"Sweet wench," sed he. "Never fret! These jerks deleyeght me. Nevertheless, when fermer peckers tempt thee, feel free, prehend them! E.g. Tencrède's. He's sheer steel!"

"Yer Emeenence's dedd sweet," Estelle repleyed. "Never feer! Elders, even senescents pleese me! Tell me whether yer Emeenence'd let secret remedees help?"

"Reel secrets?" he begged.

"Well, secret'd never be the perfect term. Severel texts reveel them."

"Then tell me!"

"These remedees've been esteemed sens the Pre-Reneysence; even these deys sex GP's tell despretте men:

when deth neers, the member erects. The best wey's when we pend the geezer.

"Pend me! We'd never seek the End!!"

"Keep serene, Emeenence. We'll pend thee, then depend thee when the member's well erected 'n' entered me!"

"Trew? The sqweeze'll erect me?"

"The Emeenence'll resemble Eyefell's Needle!"

"Yer scheme depresses me, sweetee; yet when we've screwed, the peyn'll've been well spent!"

"The Emeenence'll never regret the peyn. Beleeve me. Then releeve me!"

Tender Estelle then petted the meek, feeble member. Next, she erttempted the Reverend Excellence's pendencee. Yet neck sqweezes're never eezee peezee.

"Hey geezers! Hey gerls!" she yelled. "Help me!"

The wenches', the clerks' 'n' the geys' perverse embreyces were then ceesed. They encercled her.

The Reverend Spencer fetched lether fetters, then segmented seven excellent metres. Even then, the clerks fetched the See's step-ledder. The fetters were then fed between the beems' s-bends. They perpended freelee.

"These steps seem veree heyegh," the Reverend Excellence mewled. "Three metres' pendencee terreefeyes me!"

"Let the Emeenence erscend the steps!"

Estelle herself tethered the reverend neck.

"Set, Excellence?" she begged. Then she reversed the steps. The fetters stretched, then sqweezed the Emeenence's neck. Vertebrers wrenched, veyns reddened, the end seemed neyegh. Yet, the sqweeze's effects were the Reverend Excellence's meek member's reberth: he swelled, stretched, then erected.

When she'd seen the expected effect, Estelle spred her legs

then held the Reverend Excellence between them, wheyele the Reverend Spencer severed the fetters. The Emeenence's fresh sceptre, well-fleshed, sheer steel, entered her!

"Feed me metres!" she yelled. "Screw me senseless!"

They French-necked wheyele the Emeenence's remettled member empeyled her. He resembled Herkewelees neer Thebes; Ewelessees when he entered Crete.

The rest encercled them. The member's breef, yet vehement strength left them speechless.

"He's the greytest!"

"The verve! The mettle!"

"He's the elders' green-pecker!"

Well, extreme glee meykes men therstee. We then rested there 'n' reqwested refreshment.

"Jeez! We're desseekeyted!" yelled Thérèse 'n' Bérengère. The Reverend Spencer then led them where the freezers were.

"Perfect, eyeced refreshments!"

"Schweppes?"

"Yes pleese!"

The wey they dreyned the Schweppes seemed excesseeve. Meenwheyele, Ernest seezed the breyk's pretext, then sed re the beesness:

"Eh, Clément, re the beesness. . ."

"The beesness. . . ?"

"B de BB's necklesses, peebreyn!"

"Never fret, Ernest. Hélène's the leederene. When she reckens the theyeme's reyepe, she'll yell. Then the rest'll ensew. Cheyeld's pley!"

"Reelee, Clément! We've the perfect pretext here! Speed's the best bet. We'll detect the jewels, fleece them, then flee!"

"Keep serene! We've seen Bérengère's gemless. She's cleerlee secreted her jewels, seeled them, dessembled them 'n' the rest. Let Hélène leed, then the fleece'll be perfect!"

Ernest seemed vexed. Yet, teeth clenched, he reterned between the henchmen. Then where ley Hélène? There, her legs well spred, she expertlee keressed herself, wheyele the Reverend Spencer 'n' Tencrède jerked themselves between her brests. Between enterteynments leyeke these, she'd never heed Ernest's recent reqwests. Enywey, the rest breyks were ended. The revels reheeted.

The ephebes esseyed the clerks. They let them. They even seemed well pleesed. The Benedek brethren, Edme de Bénévent, Stephen Brewster the well-membered, Lew, Peter, Jesse, Ernest, Kenneth, René, Herbert, Celse 'n' Bebel stretched then threw themselves pell-mell, chewed, jerked, beggered, erected endless bestreddlements.

Kenneth reversed Bellfree Bebel then entered the ephebe's cheeks, meenwheyele Herbert went K9 then chewed Peter's pecker, Dédé Benedek beggered Herbert, Celse entered Stephen Brewster's teeth, then he jerked Ernest the messer's centre leg freneteeklee.

"Strewth, the clergee's the best ley," leered Lew.

Wheyele he blew René's member, he entered Edme de Bénévent's tender end. Next, Jeff 'n' Stephen Benedek went sextee-neyene then chewed there geneetles.

Even then, the Reverend Excellence-Estelle merger seemed neer the end. They needed releese. The Emeenence's seventee yeers certenlee yet seemed green. Nevertheless, the reserves weren't endless: the wey he persevered presented deep deyngers! The Excellence's flesh gleemed, members trembled repeetedlee. He seemed neer deth's derm, yet these extreme peyns never prevented renewed empressements.

"Cede, Excellence!" yelled Estelle. "Serve me the semen we seek!"

Her teeth then peerced the Emeenence's French-necker.

He bled leeters. These jets were the element he needed. The deep screws speeded, then the errth trembled! Fleet express treyns met helter-skelter; eternel sleet enswept Mégève; Mt Pelé smelted fervent sqwerts; Everest cleft! The Reverend Excellence keyme!

"We're spent! Spent!" he wheezed.

"Me leyekweyese," screeched Estelle. "He's drenched me!"

She held the Reverend Excellence neer her, then petted endless tender empressements.

Yet these excesses neerlee slew the Emeenence. He teetered, he neerlee feynted. Desprette, she held the eldster erect. Yet he enfeebled. The trembles never ceesed. He swelled. He bled. Wee yelps were herd between the reverend teeth. Estelle fetched her kleenexes, wetted them, then her tender keresses stemmed the pleyces where the Emeenence bled. She fretted. Meseemed she needed help. Her eyes drew me neer her.

"Where'll we get help, deer brer?" she begged. "The Reverend Excellence's decedent!"

"Keep serene, schwester!" she herd me repleye. "He's merelee dedd-beet. When he's rested then slept, he'll feel seventeen ergeyn!"

We reysed then settled the Emeenence. We resembled begetters when they bed there fledgelets.

"See lest the reverend pecker freeze!" yelled the Reverend Spencer, the trew dexter-member. He peered where we'd leyd the Emeenence, yet never left Hélène's brests ere he'd perl-necklessed her.

We respected Spencer's reqwest. We bedded the Excellence, nestled between tweed sheets.

Estelle cleerlee felt endebted. She next bedded me, then expertlee blew me wheyele her gentle feelers jerked me. She speeded me erect. Redressed, the feller resembled resmelted steel. She bestreddled me then, eqwestree-enne, clenched me. The scene exceyeted Bérengère 'n' Thérèse wheyele they embreyced.

Thérèse spred her legs, bent, then presented me her nether cheeks. Then she 'n' Estelle French-necked. Next, Bérengère merged between them. They petted her beever then her cheeks. The three wenches resembled heeted she-setters. Then the pecker's fervent screws felled the ensemble. Pell-mell we rekermmenced: me, eyes between Estelle's cheeks, entered Thérèse's effervescent sex k-neynlee, Bérengère then drew the testes between her teeth.

"Hey! Where's me eencest, then?" pestered Estelle. "Thérèse, let me strew the brer's seed."

Her reqwest, meseemed, vexed Thérèse.

"Where're Clément's preferences?" she begged me.

"Well, the schwester's hevvenlee cleft tempts me, yet need presses. Let Estelle cede Thérèse the seed. She'll get hers leyter!"

"Mmmm," she regretted. "Let's see whether he keeps feyth!"

The empressement nevertheless persevered. We neered the spermerment. Bérengère's testeekewele pets never ceesed, wheyele her feelers entered between the cheeks. The member swelled, resembled the Zeplen, entered then re-entered Thérèse's sex freneteeklee, wheyele teeth chewed the schwester's drenched beever. Then Thérèse flexed her theyeghs. The fervent sperm sperted.

"Néhédeen Rebbeq!" Thérèse mewled (she remembered her Berber revels). "The hevvenlee jet!"

Meseemed me veynes seethed, breyns cleft, temples berst, vertebrers lewsened, members bled wheyete. Hevven! Yet Hell seemed dedd neer.

Thérèse let me desert her, then rest. Even then, the clerks

'n' benders leyekweyese rested themselves. The Reverend Excellence slept. Hélène's brests were sew sperm-drenched, kleenexes'd never qwench her!

Tencrède, nevertheless, seemed peeved.

"Reelee!" the presser peenged. "These revels need steel! Steel's the essence! Certes, lewdness never reqweyeres restreynts. Yet here, the revels seem mere meyhem: here we screw, there we get screwed; here we jerk, there we get chewed. Yet cleverness's needed. We never reflect! We're mere beests! Esthetes, when they resemble me, regret heedlessness."

"Tencrède reflects!" jested the Reverend Spencer. "Leeve these schemes! Let's be free! Let's screw where we select. Ferget yer perverted bestreddlements. Let the revellers feel stress-free!"

Yet these entreetees nettled Tencrède.

"Stress-free! Stress-free!" he sneered. "Where's the sense? Revellers're best when they express themselves! Let the members' deeds resemble Klee when he sketched, Sceve when he penned verses, Webern when he set themes! We seek the essence where the end meets the endless! Yet Spencer here begs me let the revellers wrestle stress-free! Strewth!"

Tencrède's vehement speech set debeyte between the ensemble.

"Trencrede speeks trew," decreed Edme de Bénévent.

"Tencrède's scheme seems excellent," repeeted Lewd-End Lew.

"Leyes! Legends! Tencrède's speech's senseless!" yelled Stephen Brewster. "When men screw, they express themselves per se, perdee. Scenes when set present mere deckerdence, seneyele meyhem!"

"Yes," repleyed Bérengère. "Nevertheless, when shrewd hedds beget revels, they're the sweetest! Let Tencrède, the esthete, present then feed the scene."

"Never!" yelled Thérèse. "Lessezz fere! Let's screw!"

These speeches reysed the Reverend Excellence. Then Spencer decreed the well-esteemed Emeenence'd better settle the debeyte.

"Meseems the term 'revel'," he slerred, "meens we need reveleyshen!"

The Excellence's excellent speech re-settled the ensemble, even the rebels.

"Well, let's see," ceded Thérèse. "Meybe Tencrède's scheme's sweet."

She then let the clerk emcee the scene.

"Encercle me," yelled Tencrède. "Then heed the emcee's decrees!"

"We bend," sed Hélène. "Yer reqwests'll be respected."

"Yer the cheef," went Ernest. "The henchmen'll serve thee!"

"Denke," repleyed Tencrède. "Let me errn yer respect!"

Then seyelentlee we heeded Tencrède's emceements:

"Let ferst the esteemed, the Reverend Emeenence be sewepeyene. Then let deer sweet Bérengère bend between the emeenent legs, chew the member tenderlee, then mey she herself spred her legs, reyse her cheeks, wheyele Clément serves her k-neyenelee. Meenwheyele, the Benedek brethren's tender empressements'll resemble Greek ephebes'; they'll enter feelers between nether cheeks, erect, the Emeenence's theyeghs between them, where there feet mey kerress the reverend chest – he mey chew them whenever he pleeses – Clément's teeth'll then enterteyn the brethren's members. Next, let Kenneth Peebles sneek between Clément's legs, reyse hedd, then gentlee, expertlee chew Bérengère's beever. She'll get deleesheslee drenched! Let Kenneth's pecker then penetreyte the eqwestreene Bellfree Bebel; elsewhere, he'll eet Thérèse's pert crewp, then feel Stephen Brewster's testes. Mey Stephen screw Thérèse endlesslee. Next, let perseverent Bebel's expert feet gentlee jerk the Reverend Spencer. Mey he chew Hélène's drenched qweem, then Herbert begger her wheyele she lets her svelte deegets enter Celse's sphencter 'n' wheyele he jerks the deer brethren: Edme the dexter, René the left. Elsewhere, let Estelle steel between Celse then Ernest, let Ernest feel her, then Celse begger her. Mey Lewd-End Lew bend, leen, then chew Ernest's 'bene pendentes'. Let Peter bend between Lew's leys then chew, wheyele Jesse screws Lew k-neyenlee. Then the emcee'll begger Jesse! The scene ends here."

"We'll be the end's essence!" trembled Bérengère.

"Yes," serene Tencrède repleyed. "We'll resemble Greek see-steemers when tempests heel them."

The pleyers pleyced themselves. When he set the scene (here he resembled Welles) Tencrède's terms were breef, even severe. Yet the bestreddlements weren't eezee peezee. The henchmen never remembered Tencrède's decrees. They erred. They resembled Cerventes neer the Ebre's streems.

"Hell, they're ewesless berks!" he sneered. He helped them, led them where he'd decreed. The henchmen let themselves be led. They nevertheless seemed perplexed. We herd them excheynge secret mermers. Steeth! Where led these jesses' schemes? Wheyele Bérengère's revered, secret cercle held me ever deeper meye eyes serched Hélène 'n' Thérèse. Yet, when revels resemble these, we never see cleerlee.

Tencrède's demented erectshen nevertheless heeved. Here the geezers, there the wenches, entered, chewed, jerked, screwed between endless perverse lewdnesses. Presentlee, the set represented mere seyeghs, yerks, sperm-jets. Well, greyt! 'n' yet, Jeez, the peyn! Legs, bellee, vertebrers hert leyeke hell!

"Sweyepe me!" yelled Bellfee Bebel. "Me scent cells eetch!"

"Keep serene, Bebel!" Tencrède stressed.

He nevertheless sneezed: the excellent erectshen fell! Celse teetered. He felled Edme then René. They reversed Estelle!

We resembled feeble, wrecked belvederes when they're levelled; DC Sevens when stens fell them; bens when erthqweykes tremble them. The segmented revellers fell, then resettled themselves pell-mell.

"Here leyes these scenes' deep deynger," regretted Tencrède. "The geezer sneezes, then blews the erectshen!"

Serene Bérengère then jested (she resembled the greyt Gégène):

"Yep, see where the prester pressed her!"

Then the gerls detected me; they drew me between them.

"Ernest the messer perplexes me, Hélène. He seems streynge, eh?"

"Yes, yet where's the wretched jerk's scheme?"

"Re the jewels. . . When'll we get them?"

"Never feel pressed! We'll weyt, then, when the clerks've left. . ."

"Screw the clerks!"

"They're nevertheless 'tecs!"

"'Tecs? Never!"

"Yep. The seventh sense tells me."

"Well neet! The 'tecs're here! Then let Ernest 'n' the henchmen fleece the necklesses, the peelers'll errest them, then we'll be serene!"

"The peelers feel the benders! Excellent!" the wenches yelled.

Ernest's perverse, secret, rebel schemes'd depressed them. They then felt refettled, repepped, 'n' sed they'd screw me. The wee feller entered Hélène's cheeks, wheyele Thérèse's expert teeth pecked the pendents. Yet, when Estelle'd seen these events, she presented herself then begged me serve her the sperm she'd expected ever sens we'd sed she'd get her eencest. We settled her preference there 'n' then. Meenwheyele, Thérèse let Kenneth essey her; 'n' Hélène, Herbert.

Strewth, eencest's sweet! When we screwed we remembered the green Eden we'd sheyred: when Estelle'd terned seven, she dressed her yeller tresses; September sweltered, she devested herself, entered the streem, then beythed. Her brer ley neer the embenkment; she emerged then ley beseyede me! Then we excheynged endless sweet tendernesses: her teeth, her meek members, her svelte legs, the neer-expert cheeks' perverseness. Yes, seven yeers were extremelee tender!

When she encercled me, these remembrences' sweet smells whelmed me. Her lewd feelers kerressed me between the theyeghs, wheyele vehement me pecked her cheeks, temple, neck. Her pert, speer-leyeke brests skewered me. Then, leyeke the Eblé, when the eestern freeze meyde the French retreet, the member went berserk between her, then keyme. The frenzee releesed revenents wherever we peered!

"Begetters!" screeched Estelle. "The sperm peerces me!"

She releesed the effervescent member then, between her teeth, she bezelled the breef yet repeeted sperm-jets.

Even then, fresh effervescence welled reyefe between the clerks.

"Excellence! Excellence! When're vespers?" begged the Reverend Spencer.

"Yes, veree trew," went he.

The presters presterned themselves, wheyele he remeyned erect.

"Bérengère'll be the vessel," he decreed, "where the shepherds then the sheep'll receeve the seycrements."

Bérengère ley beseyede the Reverend Excellence. He held her legs, then reysed them. She then stretched herself.

He fetched then served the seycred red gentlee between Bérengère's legs. The clerks Q'ed, bent themselves 'n' receeved the seycrement.

Next, wheyele the Emeenence's freyl feelers kerressed seven deeveyene bedes, he sed the vespers. They weren't Geneses, they cleerlee weren't Gerspels, yet they were excellent verses:

"Heed, Seycred Redeemer, these vespers' fervent verses! Let the eencense we've esperged reech thee, let these revels' excellence encheer thee! Let the celeste spheres' sweet themes enter thee, let the endless sererpheem seed thee then reseed thee; let presents be spred, let them resemble the Bethlehem crèche's; then mey the Endless Begetter let thee enter Eden's demesne!"

"Eymen!" yelled the clerks.

Bérengère, svelteness's extreme, bent herself then bezzled the red the clerks'd left.

"Sperm's better," she cleymed. "Yet red's nevertheless excellent!"

Next, the clerks hennered members 'n' nether cheeks, encercled the henchmen then reqwested the ephebes' felleyshens.

Ernest left the pew, then decreed:

"These clergeekle excesses meyke me retch."

"Nevertheless, cheef," entervened Jesse Jeymes, "prest-Rs' felleyshens're the bees' knees!"

"Never defeye me!" yelled Ernest.

He seemed well nettled; new events seemed set between the henchmen.

"We reveyele the revels, get me?" Ernest resewemed. "Let's be cleer! We expect Bérengère's jewels eemeedetlee!"

Well, the Reverend Excellence, Bérengère 'n' the clerks

peed themselves. Yet we knew Ernest never jested. There 'n' then, the jerk's Beretter erppeered. The speed he'd ewesed seemed spell-leyeke!

Serenelee Lewd-End Lew redressed, then seezed the stens he'd secreted. Next, the rest leyekweyese redressed. We were encercled; the exets defended.

We were wretched, the clerks, the wenches 'n' me. The Reverend Excellence went grey, the Reverend Spencer green, the perplexed clerks' peckers weelted. The wenches seemed well vexed. Yet they'd see me keep serene, 'n' expect the peelers' entrence. Nevertheless, Ernest then seemed the leeder. The stens we'd dessembled weren't neer me.

"These events deeplee depress me," sed the Reverend Excellence serenelee.

"The Beretter's restless, Excellence!" yelled Ernest.

The Reverend Excellence fell speechless. Meseemed he'd freeze: the feeble members trembled freneteklee. The Reverend Spencer esseyed defence:

"Let me get the sheets then shelter the Emeenence. See where he trembles!"

"Get them, 'n' we'll get thee!" sneered Ernest.

Bérengère nevertheless seemed fereless; she even pretended these events pleesed her.

"When'll Ernest get clever?" she jeered. "He resembles senseless weyns! He'll cleerlee get stewed! Where's the jerk's hedd?"

"Sh, Bérengère," went the Reverend Excellence. "The wretch here's rewthless!"

"Sheyete!" she repleyed. "Ernest merelee needs breyns. Pretend he'll get the necklesses! Perfect fecklessness! Never beleeve the berk!"

Meseemed he'd never even herd her. He smeyeled then sneered:

"Yer dedd sweet, Bérengère. The cleverest! We merelee seek the gems. Yet we'll let thee select deth! Where's yer preference?"

"We repeet, then rerepeet: yer the greenest nerd we've ever met!"

"Jeez, the wench peeves me!" went Lew.

"Let her beever. Then screw her!" Ernest repleyed. "We nevertheless expect the jewels."

"Well, then get them!"

"Perfect!"

"They're secreted between the den's recesses," sed Bérengère serenelee.

Ernest, meseemed, reflected deep:

"Hey, the Benedeks! Leed her where she sleeps then redescend when she's reveeled the gems!"

The gemels left. They steered Bérengère between them.

Weeks, semesters even, crept beye. The clerks excheynged weenks. Hélène, Thérèse, even Estelle seemed well serene. The Reverend Excellence's teeth, eyes 'n' eers were clensed. Ernest 'n' the henchmen peeped 'n' peered whenever they expected the Benedeks' retern.

"Where're the bleeders?" Ernest mermered.

Hmmm, let me see, the hedd debeyted: Bérengère'd cleerlee beeten the Benedeks. There were Jesse, Peter, Bebel, Lew, Ernest then the Beretters left. The Beretters were the key! When we need stens, then we get ledded. Streyt sets!

"Hey, Ernest! Meseems the men'll never redescend!" jeered Hélène. Here she resembled Bérengère. She despeyesed Ernest. He fell speechless; seemed perplexed.

"Ernest's stewed when he demeens Bérengère's deftness," she perseested. "She'll fell endless men when they resemble the Benedek berks!"

"Meseems she speeks trew," went the Reverend Spencer.

115

"Shet there beeks! Shet there beeks!" screeched Jesse, well nettled.

"Keep serene, feller," went Ernest. "Never fret! Let Peter 'n' Bebel fetch me the Benedeks."

Nerds, yet well-treyned nerds, they yessed then left. There were merelee Jesse, Lew then Ernest left!

The jerk seemed well dense! We'd never seen twerps persevere between errers when they resembled Ernest's. The few nerds yet left seemed deyzed, feelers pressed neer the Beretters' treegers. We, nether cheeks clenched, nevertheless fretted: where led these geezers' schemes? Revenge? Merder the wenches? The Reverend Excellence? Me? Creyzee! Yet merder resembled these degenereytes. There we were, defenceless. We expected the werst.

"Hm! Hm!" hemmed the Reverend Spencer.

"Qweye-et!" yelled Ernest.

When the Reverend Spencer'd seen me bend sleyeghtlee, sew sleyeghtlee Ernest never detected me, he descrreetlee reysed the sheets neer where the Reverend Excellence'd been bedded. Benneeth them were steel chenets!

Tee hee! Trew, we'd never get them eezeelee. Yet when we'd fetched them, we'd bewelter Ernest 'n' the henchmen. Then we'd be free!

Feet, then feelers helped me eeze, sleether the chenets neerer the clerks then me. The wey they sleyeded resembled serpents between herbs. Meenwheyele, the wenches keened streyedent eres. Ernest 'n' the henchmen hence'd never detect the scheme.

"Seyelence! Seyelence!" Ernest screeched.

"Let's shet the wenches' beeks, they're demented!" yelled Lew.

"Let's belt them! Skewer them! Then they'll ceese!" went Jesse.

The chenets'd then neerlee reeched Edme de Bénévent, Stephen Brewster 'n' me. We bent then clenched them.

"Hm! Hm!" rehemmed the Reverend Spencer.

Ere Ernest'd herd these hems, we breyvlee threw the chenets: Edme selected Lew, Stephen Jeff, they left me Ernest the messer. These express-speed chenets left them Beretterless. Hedds belted, they teetered, then fell. The clerks then eezeelee fettered them.

Meseemed these events' term never penetreyted Ernest's hedd. Then, sereneness herself, Bérengère redescended 'n' sed the Benedek brethren, Peter Pence 'n' Bellfree Bebel were leyekweyese netted! These nerds'd been led between the peelers she knew encercled the dens.

"We're blessed these rebels were trew twerps!" the Reverend Spencer jested.

"We're pleesed," decreed the Reverend Excellence. "These fell events' term seems perfect! We'll re-esperge the Endless Redeemer. Let's remember Bérengère's expert deftness! Then Clément's, Stephen's 'n' Edme's speed! Yet ferget the sermens! Redeemer's speed! Let the revels retern. Then we'll resemble the Pheenex, when these ehshes represent lewd verve's reberth, then engender rewd scenes, endless perverse sketches!"

Then Hélène herd me kermpleyn:

"Then we're stewed! Beggered!"

"Well, the teyeme never seems reyepe," she repleyed. "We'll see. These excesses'll certenlee engender deep sleep. We'll then serenelee leeve then fetch Bérengère's jewels."

"Yes, we'll see. Nevertheless, meseems we've been checked..."

"Never despeyre, deer brer," went Estelle. "Hélène reezens well."

"Then be reserved," Hélène resewemed. "Never get

exerted, lest we leyekweyese sleep when the reel beesness kermences!"

Meenwheyele, Ernest 'n' the henchmen felt the clerks' vengence. The Reverend Spencer fetched elm fleyls then beweltered Lew 'n' Jesse, wheyele the Reverend Excellence selected the chenets then, leyeke terebrers, entered them between Ernest's cheeks. The geezers screeched. The clerks seemed dedd pleesed. Yet Bérengère pestered them:

"Reelee! Yer mere jewveneyeles! We feel leyeke the frenzeed Qween, when endless men'd entered her, then she'd seen them ejected between Nesle's crenelled defences!"

"Tee hee!" went the Reverend Excellence. "The Reneyssence, eh? Revels', plejers' trew peek!"

"They were mere lewd lechers!" sed Tencrède.

The clerks seemed well exceyeted. They expressed perverse preferences:

"We'll resemble Verres," Kenneth decreed, "when he went drenched between seven hendred 'n' seventee-seven wellbled serfs' sperm!"

"Let's get well-pendented neeggers!" went Bérengère.

"Let's see Gretchens when they sqwerm!"

"Keeddees! Wee nether cheeks!"

"Teethless shrews!"

"Reyepened wenches, Mrs Beeten!"

"Red setters!"

"Red setters?" yelled the Reverend Excellence. "We're dense! We've endless setters, teckels etc. Reverend Spencer!"

"Yes, Excellence?"

"Ceese the wey yew welter these senseless ephebes, then get me Neree the teckel 'n' Erèbe the red setter."

"Yes, Emeenence, we'll speed!"

The Reverend Spencer left, then eemmeedetlee reterned. He led the k-neyenes. Stephen, Kenneth 'n' Tencrède seezed

Bérengère then spred her legs. Celse 'n' Herbert fetched Erèbe, then vehementlee jerked the setter's member. Bérengère screeched when the well-erected setter entered her then shed leeters.

"Setters reelee send her?" Thérèse herd me reqwest.

"She detests them," Thérèse repleyed. "Yet she's fervent when the sweet Excellence's here!"

These seeds engendered the tempest. Endless perverse schemes entered the lechers' hedds. The clerks descended between trew lewdness's extremes. The presters held Jesse, wheyele the Reverend Excellence – he resembled trew senescence – excremented between the ephebe's teeth, then meyde Jesse chew the werms left between the cleft. Lew reeled then went green wheyele the clerks let fleye endless fell nether breezes. They then merged pell-mell: excrement 'n' sperm smeered chests, legs, temples, cheeks, eyes, members...

The Reverend Spencer erred between these enmeshed clerks 'n' bewELtered them. Bérengère's teets fed the Reverend Excellence; he resembled new-weened beybes. Yet she never ceesed her setter-jerks...They were wretched, fell, cheerless...

Yet then these deep effervescences' effects were felt. The frenzee ended. Bérengère wheezed. She seemed neer deth. The clerks teetered then wept feeblee. The scene resembled Sheykspeere's pleys' ends: eech pleyer decedent.

"Gerls!" they herd me decree. "Let's get the jewels!"

Perfect seyelence reyned when we left these perverse revels' fell stench. Deep greyness sheltered the See. Meseemed the peelers'd left. We eezeelee detected Bérengère's den.

"Well, where're the jewels?" begged Thérèse.

"Let's see."

The keys were eezee meet; they were there neer the bedsted.

"Then where's Bérengère's rewse?"

"Here! We see! Remember 'The Fleeced Letters'? The best secret's when we leeve the key reveeled!"

Yes endeed, the keys releesed the shelves' defences, then depenned the chests, where the gems were dessembled: perls, breycelets, necklesses etc...

"Phew! The reel leedle erner!"

There we were, the scheme ended, the werk settled. Then, sleyeghtlee wrecked, yet cheered, deleyeghted, Hélène, Thérèse, Estelle 'n' me resembled the Three Mewsketeers. We seezed the gems then left the See. We re-emerged when Exeter yet remeyned grey-flecked then, serene, the jet flew thence where sweet Frenchness beckened.

THE END

A GALLERY PORTRAIT

Georges Perec

A GALLERY PORTRAIT
The Story of a Painting

Translated by Ian Monk

A VERBA MUNDI BOOK
DAVID R. GODINE · *Publisher* · *Boston*

INTRODUCTION

DAVID BELLOS

Like Perec's masterpiece, *Life A User's Manual*, *A Gallery Portrait* is a description of a painting. It seems to have been inspired by a 3,000-piece jigsaw representing a painting by W. van Haecht entitled *A Visit to a Gallery*. The puzzle's box can be seen propped up on the mantelpiece of Perec's flat in Rue Linne, in a photograph taken in October 1978 for the press launch of *Life A User's Manual*.

A Gallery Portrait confirms Perec's increasing interest in the visual arts at that stage in his career, and in optical as well as textual deceptions. It is a kind of jigsaw puzzle in its construction, as it is made up at least in part of fragments of other texts, of allusions to other works, most notably to *Life A User's Manual*, and of personal nods and winks to friends and to places associated with them. For example, "Ursule Boulou" (p. 171) is the name of a cat belonging to close friends; and *St Wendel Station*, an imaginary painting described on p. 150, beautifies an ugly modern building on a branch-line near Saarbrucken that Perec had had occasion to visit and to joke about with his German friends. *A Gallery Portrait* seems designed to tease the reader into a tracking and hunting game, essentially in the rest of Perec's oeuvre, in search of sources or connections that might "explain" the pieces. But as there is no real end to the game – no solution to the overall puzzle – readers may just as well enjoy the pleasure of being deceived.

A Gallery Portrait is the last complete book that Perec wrote before his death at the age of 46 in 1982. The theme of forgery, which is at its centre, is also the subject of Perec's first and still unpublished novel, *Le Condottiere* (1960). A thoroughly constructed and perplexing pendant to *Life A User's Manual*, *A Gallery Portrait* magnifies the image that Perec liked to give of himself in his youth as well as in maturity, that of a would-be painter working with words – like the painter Serge Valene, the narrator of *Life A User's Manual*, who left only a blank canvas, together with a plan for telling an infinite number of stories.

For Antoinette and Michel Binet

There I saw canvases of the greatest value, most of which I had admired in private collections in Europe and at art exhibitions. The various schools of Old Masters were represented by a Madonna by Raphael, a Virgin by Leonardo da Vinci, a nymph by Correggio, a woman by Titian, an Adoration by Veronese, an Assumption by Murillo, a portrait by Holbein, a monk by Velásquez, a martyr by Ribera, a village fair by Rubens, two Flemish landscapes by Teniers, three small *genre* paintings by Gerard Dou, Metsu and Paulus Potter, two canvases by Géricault and Prud'hon, some seascapes by Backhuysen and Vernet. Among the modern works of art figured paintings signed by Delacroix, Ingres, Decamps, Troyon, Meissonier, Daubigny, etc.

JULES VERNE
Twenty Thousand Leagues under the Sea

A GALLERY PORTRAIT, by Heinrich Kürz, the American painter of German origin, was displayed in public for the first time in 1913 in Pittsburgh, Pennsylvania, during a series of cultural events which the town's German community had organized to mark the twenty-fifth anniversary of the reign of Kaiser Wilhelm II. Under the triple auspices of the daily newspaper *Das Vaterland*, of the Amerikanische Kunstgesellschaft and of the German-American Chamber of Commerce ballets, concerts, fashion parades, trade and food fairs, industrial shows, gymnastic displays, art exhibitions, plays, operas, operettas, variety shows, lectures, grand balls and banquets followed one another without interruption for several months, thus giving those Germanophiles that had flooded in from the four corners of the American continent the opportunity to see ever more ambitious productions. The three linchpins of the series were undoubtedly an open-air performance of an uncut *Faust Part Two* (which was unfortunately interrupted by the rain after seven and a half hours), the world première of Manfred B. Gottlieb's oratorio, *Amerika*, the performance of which required two hundred and twenty-five musicians, eleven soloists and eight hundred choristers, and the first Pittsburgh performance of *Das Gelingen*, a startling operetta which had been especially brought over from Munich, along with its two famous original leads, Theo Schuppen and Maritza Schellenbube.

Amid these lavish productions, with their eye-grabbing advertisements which took up entire pages of magazines, the exhibition of paintings, held in the suites of the Bavaria Hotel from April until October, almost went by unnoticed. The Pittsburgh press had much less to say about the paintings and artists than about the personalities that attended the official opening: Senator Lindemann, Judge Taviello, the steel magnate Kellogg O'Brien, the millionaire Barry O. Fugger, owner and managing director of Fugger department stores, and the forty-three members of the German delegation led by Dr Ulrich Schultze, First Under-Secretary of the Imperial Chancellory and His Majesty's special envoy. As for the art critics in America's German-language press, they were generally content just to list a few artists' names and the titles of a few paintings, sometimes rounding them off with brief, general-purpose commentaries: In the "Still-Life" section, we particularly admired Garten's *Teapot on a Table*, whose palette shows an admirable mastery of all the shades of blue, a very fine *Fruit Dish*, from the brush of the late regretted Sigmund Becker and James Zapfen's *Workbench*, whose rather heavy-handed realism seems to have been tempered by some unstated tenderness, and so on.

In this rather unfavourable context, Kürz's work was hardly better treated than the rest, even if, with the benefit of hindsight, we can today remark that it received quite flattering notices: Anton Zweig, in the *Chicago Tagblatt*, described it as being a "strange Poe-like painting, which will surely cause much ink to be spilt"; Walther Bannerträger, in the brief review he sent to the *New York Zeitung*, regretted that he could "mention only in passing [this] subtly symbolic portrait, whose highly metaphysical inspiration must put a question mark over much of what received opinion considers to constitute Beauty in Art"; Christian von Muschelsohn, of the Milwaukee *Morgenstern*, saw in it "a muffled exaltation of new Nietzschean values, reinvesting the whole of the visible and invisible world"; while the article in the *Vaterland*, written by one of the exhibition's organizers, Thadeus Doppelgleisner, was notably fuller (perhaps because the painting's owner, Hermann Raffke, of Raffke Breweries, had loaned several works to the exhibition and had generously contributed to its financing) but it still remained firmly fixed in the realm of generalities and gossip:

Our eminent fellow-townsman Hermann Raffke, from Lübeck, is not only famous for the excellent beer he has been successfully brewing in our town for almost fifty years, but is also an enlightened and enthusiastic artlover who is well known in art galleries and studios on both sides of the Atlantic. During his many trips to Europe, Hermann Raffke's eclectic and sound discernment has allowed him to build up an entire collection of ancient and modern works of art, which many a museum in the Old World would dearly like to have acquired and which is at present unparalleled in our fledgling nation, if Messrs Mellon, Kress, Duveen and the Johnsons will pardon my saying so. What is more, Hermann Raffke has always kept the development of American painting close to his heart and many now famous names, such as Thomas Harrison, Kitzenjammer, Wyckoff, Betkowski and the list goes on, were backed during their early years by his discreet and generous patronage. But Hermann Raffke has chosen the occasion of this exhibition to give us the most startling proof of his threefold attachment to painting, to our town and to Germany, by commissioning the young painter Heinrich Kürz, who, we are proud to point out, was born in Pittsburgh of Wurtemburg parentage, to paint a portrait depicting him sitting in his private gallery in front of his favourite pictures. And it goes without saying that many of those very favourites come from our beautiful country, etc.

Despite the organizers' rather gloomy predictions, a few days after the official opening the exhibition became an everincreasing success and this was undoubtedly down to Heinrich Kürz's painting. This consecration of his work – and, thanks to it, of the entire exhibition – no doubt arose from some strange word-of-mouth process, the exact effects of which are always difficult to gauge, but it is perhaps possible to find an initial explanation for such enthusiasm in the long, anonymous notice published in the catalogue:

The canvas represents a large, rectangular room, without any apparent doors or windows, with its three visible walls completely covered with paintings.

To the left of the foreground, a cut-glass decanter and a wine-glass stand on a small occasional table, decked with a lace tablecloth; beside it, a man sits in an armchair, upholstered in dark-green leather, with his back at a three-quarters angle to the viewer. The man is old, with abundant white hair, a thin nose with steel-rimmed spectacles. We guess more than we can really see about his facial features: his blotchy cheek, his thick mustache drooping down well over his upper lip, his strong bony chin. He wears a grey dressing-gown, with a broad collar decorated with thin red piping. A large dog with a short reddish coat, partly concealed by the arm of the chair and by the table, lies apparently asleep at his feet.

More than one hundred paintings have been gathered together on this one canvas, reproduced so faithfully and meticulously that it would be impossible for us to describe them all in detail. Even listing their titles and artists would not only be a wearisome task, but also lie beyond the scope of this short article. Suffice it to say that all the styles of all the European and recent American schools have been superbly represented, from religious subjects to *genre* paintings, from portraits to still-lifes, from landscapes to seascapes and so on, and we shall leave to the visitor the pleasure of discovering, of recognizing and of identifying the Longhi or the Delacroix, the Gherardo of the Night or the Vernet, the Holbein or the Mattei, as well as other masterpieces worthy of Europe's greatest museums which Raffke the collector, following the sound advice of the most eminent art experts, has been able to acquire during his travels.

While refraining from going into further details, we should nevertheless like to draw the visitor's attention to three works which, we believe, bear witness as much to Raffke's good fortune in his choices, as to Heinrich Kürz's talent in depicting them.

The first, on the left-hand wall, above the collector's head, is a *Visitation* which could, as far as we are concerned, be easily attributed to some Paris Bordone, Lorenzo Lotto or Sebastiano del Piombo: in the middle of a small square, surrounded by high columns with richly embroidered hangings draped between them, the Virgin, dressed in dark-green robes, partly obscured by a long red veil, kneels before Saint Elizabeth who, old and tottering, has come up in front of her, supported by two serving-women. In the foreground, to the right, are three old men, entirely dressed in black; two of them are standing, almost facing each other; the first holds in front of him a half-unfolded piece of parchment, on which the plan of a fortified town has been traced with a thin blue line, while the second points at it with a long, bony finger; the third is sitting on a gilded wooden stool, its legs forming a cross, which is covered with a green cushion; his back is almost entirely turned to his companions and he seems to be looking into the background of the scene: a vast esplanade where Mary's escort awaits her: a closed litter with leather curtains, borne by two white horses, which two page-boys in red-and-gray livery hold by their bridles, and a knight-at-arms whose lance is decked with a long golden pennon. A landscape of hills and groves can be made out on the horizon and, in the distance, the misty towers of a city.

The second picture hangs on the right-hand wall. It is a small still-life by Chardin, entitled *Luncheon Preparations*: a ham wrapped up in a white linen cloth, a pan full of milk, a bowl of vineyard peaches and a large slice of salmon on a plate turned facedown have been laid out on a stone table amid various kitchen and household utensils: a mortar, a ladle, a skimmer, etc. Above them, a slaughtered duck hangs on the wall by a thin piece of rope, threaded through its right foot. It seems to us that Chardin's freshness, simplicity and realism have rarely been displayed with such success and we can only wonder which to admire more, the French painter's genius, or the perfect way that Kürz has "rendered" it.

Finally, while evoking this unique collection of works of art, it would seem a pity not to mention a painting that has not been placed on one of the walls, but on an easel in the right-hand corner of the gallery. It is the *Portrait of Bronco McGinnis*, he who claimed to be "The Most Tattooed Man in the World" and who exhibited himself as such at the Chicago International Exposition (after his death in 1902 it was learnt that he was a Breton, called Le Marech', and only the tattoos on his chest were genuine). This portrait is the work of one of our compatriots, Adolphus Kleidröst, who started his career in Cologne and has since brilliantly pursued it in Cleveland. It hence figures in our exhibition (see no. 95) alongside various other works from the German-American school belonging to the Hermann Raffke Collection, which have been loaned to us as well. Many visitors will no doubt care to compare the original works with the scrupulous reductions Heinrich Kürz has made of them. And here they are in for a wonderful surprise: for the artist has put his painting in the painting, so that the art collector, sitting in his gallery, has in his line of sight, on the far wall, the painting which represents himself looking at his collection of paintings, then all of the paintings themselves reproduced again without any loss of precision through the first, second and third reflections, until they are nothing more than minute brush-strokes on the canvas. *A Gallery Portrait* is not just the anecdotic depiction of a private collection, it is also, in its play of succeeding reflections and in the near-magical charm that these increasingly minuscule repetitions create, a work of art which tips us into its own oneiric universe where its power of seduction has been amplified to an infinite degree and where the agonizing precision of the medium, far from being an end in itself, suddenly opens out into the vertiginous spirituality of the Eternal Return.

By the second week, the room where Heinrich Kürz's picture had been hung became so crowded that the organizers found themselves obliged to let in only twenty-five visitors at a time and to make them leave again after quarter of an hour. This room had been arranged, as an additional refinement, to recreate Hermann Raffke's gallery as accurately as possible. *A Gallery Portrait* took up all of the far wall and the *Portrait of Bronco McGinnis* was positioned on its easel in the right-hand corner; the only other pictures displayed in the room also came from the Raffke Collection and were arranged on the walls in positions corresponding to those which they occupied in Kürz's painting.

Nobody ever seemed to tire of comparing the originals with Kürz's tinier and tinier reproductions. People soon began amusing themselves by working out that the painting's format was a little under three metres, by a little over two, that the first "painting in the painting" was still almost a metre long by seventy centimetres high, that the third measured only eleven centimetres by eight, that the fifth was smaller than a postage stamp and that the sixth measured barely five millimetres by three. The day after some fellow equipped with a jeweller's glass climbed onto the shoulders of two mates and declared that even here you could see very precisely the seated man, the easel with the portrait of the tattooed man, and then again the painting with the seated man, and then one last time the painting reduced to a thin line no more than half a millimetre long, several dozen visitors came with every kind of magnifying and weaver's glasses, setting off a cult that caused the businesses of every optical-equipment supplier in the city to boom for several months.

These crazed observers would come back several times a day in order to examine systematically every square inch of the painting, using a wealth of ingenuity (or daring acrobatics) to try to get a better look at the upper reaches of the canvas. Their favourite sport was spotting the differences between the various versions of the works it depicted, at least through the first three reproductions, after which most of the details were obviously no longer discernible. One might have thought that the painter would have done his utmost to make his copies as faithful as possible and that any noticeable modifications had been forced on him by the very limits of his technical abilities. But, on the contrary, it soon became clear that he had made a point of never exactly re-copying his models and that he seemed to have taken a mischievous delight in introducing some slight variation in each of them: figures, details vanished from one copy to the next, or changed places, or were replaced by others: the teapot in Garten's painting became a blue enamel coffee-pot; a boxing champion, still in fine fettle in the first copy, was receiving a terrible upper-cut in the second, and was lying flat out in the third; carnival masks (in Longhi's *Party at the Quarli Palace*) filled up a small piazza which had initially been empty; a veiled woman, a little ass and a dromedary vanished one after the other from a Moroccan landscape; a painting depicting *Eskimos Going down the River Hamilton*, by Schönbraun, was replaced first by Dietrich Hermannstahl's *Pearl Fishers*, then by R. Mutt's *Portrait of the Bride*; the shepherd bringing home his sheep (*The Painting Lesson*,

Dutch school) could count ten of them in the first copy, twenty in the second, and none at all in the third; a lute player became a flute player (*Tavern Scene*, Flemish school); three men on a country lane went from a stoutness that verged on obesity to being almost unnervingly thin, and so on.

These imponderable and unforeseeable modifications generally affected minute details – the rather ruined black plume in a hat, two rows of pearls instead of three, the colour of a ribbon, the shape of a pan, the handle of a sword, the design of a chandelier – but they whipped up the curiosity of the visitors, whose stubborn attempts at exactly enumerating them were as vain as their attempts at grasping their initial purpose. Despite the very strict regulations imposed by the organizers to try to limit the lengths of the visits, increasingly compact groups of people with entry-passes and every other kind of queue-jumper would break the guards' vigilance and stand there for hours on end, their noses pressed against the canvas, feverishly taking notes and going through the same inaccurate calculations ten times over. The nearer the end of the exhibition came, the harder it got to make them budge an inch and soon arguments and fights broke out, to such an extent that on the evening of October 24th, less than one week before the closure, the inevitable finally happened: an exasperated visitor, who had been waiting all day without being able to get into the room, suddenly burst in and threw the contents of a large bottle of Indian ink over the painting, managing to make his getaway before he was lynched.

The next morning, the room was empty. A notice pinned up where the painting had been hung explained that, in accordance with Mr Hermann Raffke's strict instructions, *A*

Gallery Portrait as well as all the other canvases from his collection had been withdrawn from the exhibition.

A few weeks after this incident, which the press was unanimous in calling grotesque, but which cast a shadow over the last days of the exhibition (most of the artists withdrew their canvases in solidarity with the "affronted collector and artist", and the awards ceremony had to be cancelled), a long study of Kürz's painting appeared in a little-known artistic review, the *Bulletin of the Ohio School of Arts*. Its author, a certain Lester K. Nowak, called his article "Art and Reflection". "Any work of art is the mirror of another," he claimed in his introduction: the true signication of many, if not all, paintings lies in their relationship with previous works, which are either simply reproduced within them, partly or entirely, or else, in a much more allusive manner, are encoded. Particular attention should hence be given to that style of painting which is generally called "gallery portraits" ("*cabinets d' amateur*" or "*kuntskammer*"), a tradition which arose in Antwerp at the end of the sixteenth century and which continued unbroken across the main European schools of painting until around the middle of the nineteenth century. In conjunction with the very idea of museums and, naturally, that of paintings as marketable property, the initial point of these "gallery portraits" was to base the act of painting on a "reflexive dynamic", drawing its strength from the paintings of others.

Basing himself on this theory, which was rather clumsily set forward in his six-page introduction, the author went on to describe some of the better-known "gallery portraits" or "pictures in pictures": Abel Grimmer's *Christ in the House of Martha and Mary*, which contains a *Tower of Babel* by Pieter Brueghel the Elder; the series of the so-called "five senses" by Jan "Velvet" Brueghel, in which one can find works by Rubens, Van Noort, Snyders, Seghers and "Velvet" Brueghel; the countless "*kammer*" by the Francken family, in which all of Antwerp's artistic specialities are represented: Pieter Neefs's church interiors, Joos de Momper's mountain landscapes, Mostaert's conflagrations, Adam Willaerts's seascapes, "Velvet" Brueghel's nosegays, Brouwer's tavern scenes, Snyders's still-lifes, Jan Fyt's hunting trophies and so on; Wilhelm van Haecht's *Gallery Portrait of Cornelis van der Geest During the Visit of the Archduke Albert and the Archduchess Isabelle*, in which the group of personalities includes Ladislas Sigismond the King of Poland, the Burgermeister Nicolaes Rockox, Rubens, Van Dyck, Pieter Stevens, Jan Wildens, Frans Snyders and Wilhelm van Haecht himself, a melancholy-looking young man walking up the few steps that lead into his patron's gallery, in which he has reproduced a good forty pictures, including Jan van Eyck's *Woman at her Dressing Table*, which has since been lost; David Teniers the Younger's series of the *Picture Galleries of the Archduke Leopold-Wilhelm*, most of whose paintings are now in Vienna; Giovanni Paolo Pannini's *Picture Galleries*; *L'Enseigne de Gersaint*, in which Watteau, knowing that this would be his artistic testament, chose to reproduce the works he most admired; Adrien de Lelie's *The Collector Jan Gildemeester in his Gallery of Paintings*; and so on.

Lester Nowak then made a detailed analysis of Heinrich Kürz's painting showing how, while respecting Hermann Raffke's commission, the young artist had conceived a work which was in itself a veritable "history of art": "from Pisanello to Turner, from Cranach to Corot, from Rubens to Cézanne"; how he had set the continuity of the European tradition against his own development by including in his picture various works from the American (and German-

American) school from which he had directly emerged; and how, last but not least, he had put a double emphasis on the aesthetic importance of this reflection on his position as an artist, firstly by placing the very picture he had been commissioned to paint in the middle of his canvas (as though Hermann Raffke, when looking at his collection could therein see the painting representing himself looking at his collection, or, rather, as if Heinrich Kürz himself, while painting a picture representing a collection of paintings, could therein see the picture he was in the process of painting, a simultaneous end and beginning, a painting in a painting and the painting of the painting), "an infinite play of mirrors where, as in *Las Meniñas* or in Rigaud's *Self-Portrait* in the Perpignan Museum, the act of looking and what is being looked at constantly confront each other and become confused"; and secondly by including at the second, third and nth level of reflection another two of his own paintings, one an early work which Raffke had purchased from him some years before, the other a long projected work, but which was still at a preliminary stage, and whose "fictional reproduction" was "just tiny", as though it were "the anticipation of its future completion".

What had aroused the almost morbid fascination which had surrounded the work was not so much the artist's technical skill, but this spatial, and at the same time temporal, perspective. For, Lester Nowak concluded, there could be no mistake about it. This work was an image of the death of art, a mirror-reflection on this world which is condemned to an infinite reproduction of its own models. As for those slight variations from one copy to another, which had so exacerbated the visitors' curiosity, they could well be the ultimate expression of the artist's melancholia: as though, while painting the history of his own works through the history of other artists' works, he had momentarily been able to make a presence of disturbing the "established order", thus reaching an inventiveness transcending enumeration, a flash of inspiration transcending citation and a freedom transcending memory. Perhaps the work contained nothing more poignant and more laughable than the portrait of that monstrously tattooed man, that painted body which seemed to stand guard over each backward shift in the picture: man become painting under the collector's stare, a symbol which was both nostalgic and absurd, ironic and disillusioned, of that "creator" who had lost his ability to paint and who was now doomed to looking on and making a spectacle of the only thing he had left: an entirely painted surface.

On the morning of Thursday, April 2nd 1914, Hermann Raffke was found dead. His funeral took place a week later and conformed to the precise instructions he had left in his will, which were to enlarge on some of Lester Nowak's analyses in rather a macabre way. His body was mounted by the finest taxidermist of the day, brought in especially from Mexico, was clad in the same grey dressing-gown with red piping which he was wearing in Kürz's painting, then positioned in the same armchair in which he had posed. The armchair and corpse were then taken down to a cellar which faithfully reproduced, though on a much smaller scale, the room where Raffke had hung his favourite paintings. Heinrich Kürz's vast canvas took up the entire far wall. The deceased was placed in front of the picture in a position which exactly matched the one he occupied within it. To the right of the picture, in the place corresponding to the *Portrait of Bronco McGinnis*, a full-length portrait of Hermann Raffke himself was positioned on an easel. It had been painted some forty years previously while the brewer was staying in Egypt and showed him standing, with an oasis in the background, dressed in an impeccably white flannel suit, his shins done up in grey linen gaiters and wearing a pith helmet. Then the cellar was sealed up.

The first Raffke Sale took place at the Sudelwerk Gallery in Pittsburgh a few months after the collector's death. Art-lovers came in droves, impatient to see the originals of the works which, with the exception of certain German-American paintings also displayed at the exhibition, they knew only as meticulous copies in Heinrich Kürz's *A Gallery Portrait*. But they were soon disappointed. The auction catalogue featured none of the canvases which had been reproduced in Kürz's painting. Most of the works on sale belonged to the American school and, despite their high quality compared with what generally came onto the market, they aroused little enthusiasm among the buyers, who were clearly too used to this style of painting and particularly frustrated at not being able to bid furiously against one another for such and such an Old Master. Of the two hundred and sixteen lots in the catalogue, only eight went for more than one thousand dollars. Five of them were American paintings:

No. 35: *Non-Commissioned Officers During the Civil War*, by Daisy Burroughs. The relatively high price ($1,250) paid for this rather flat, naturalistic picture can no doubt be explained by the small number of works left by the artist, one of the few women to try to make a career as a painter of historical subjects. Born in 1840, a pupil of Henry Runner from 1856 to 1861, she was in Richmond in 1865 when it was under siege from the forces of General Grant. She was killed by a falling chimney pot during a storm on the night of March 19/20th.

No. 62: *Oil Wells near Forel's Fields*, by Russel Johnson. An absolutely conventional painting, but with a subject that always attracted a large clientele. It was purchased for $1,175 on behalf of a vice-president of the Amoco Motor Oil Company.

No. 72: *Natives in the Solomon Islands*, by Thomas Corbett. A member of the Squirrel Brothers' ethnographic mission, Thomas Corbett brought back a good fifty drawings and watercolours from the Solomon Islands. He then used them to construct the series of twelve large paintings that he donated to the Flora Vierkoffer Foundation, which had generously financed the expedition. Eleven of these paintings were entirely destroyed by the fire that devastated the Foundation in 1896. The twelfth, badly damaged, became part of the Raffke Collection under circumstances which have never been completely elucidated. All of which goes to explain, no doubt, why such a clumsy, academic work should find a buyer at the totally unjustifiable price of $7,200.

No. 73: *Charles M. Murphy Attempting the Mile Record on June 30th 1899*, by Bernie Bickford. Born in Buffalo, where his father worked as an engraver, Bernie Bickford's extreme precocity made him famous: he was only sixteen when he painted this picture. At the time of the auction he was in Europe, working in Bonnat's studio. Some years later, he met a notorious gangster, Angelo Merisi, on the steamer which was bringing him back to the United States. He was taken under his wing and soon became the New York underworld's confirmed portrait painter. Two of his extremely rare portraits can today be seen in the Brooklyn Police Academy Museum: one of Bunny Salvatori and one of Silvano Fiorentini, a right-hand-man of Al Capone.

No. 76: *A Squaw*, by Walker Goosetail. Of the twenty-five or so works dealing with Indian subjects in Hermann Raffke's collection, this was the only one that had any real artistic merit. Put up for sale at $300, it quickly reached $1,200, thus confirming this painter's rapidly rising reputation. It depicted a young Indian widow sitting at the foot of a totem pole, from which her husband's war trophies are hanging, and it had several similarities to Joseph Wright of Derby's famous picture of the same subject. The other three works were the only ones that came from Europe and the bidding they provoked was much more lively.

The first – No. 8 in the catalogue – was more of a curio than a work of art. It was a handle-cranked panorama, which had evidently been painted to serve as a backdrop in a puppet theatre. It consisted of a rectangular wooden frame, about sixty-five centimetres by forty, with rollers on either side for turning the canvas.

The first scene started on the banks of a canal flanked by poplars, passed by a lock, alongside some barges loaded with gravel, some fishermen with their lines, then plunged into a forest of dark trees, in the midst of which stood a hut made of logs, it then emerged onto a pathway which gradually became a street in a large town, with its many-storeyed buildings and shops selling stoneware and tiles; then the houses became more widely spaced, the sky lightened and the street became a small road in a hot country, near an oasis, where an Arab in a large straw hat trotted along on a donkey, and near a fortalice where a detachment of spahis was presenting arms; then came the sea and, after a short crossing, the scene arrived at a large harbour, went along the docks, which were drowned in mist, and entered a cold, dismal café.

A thin white band then broke the continuity of the drawing, doubtlessly to indicate that the next act was to begin. The next series of sets started in a carpenter's shop, its walls covered with saws and files, before going into the luxuriously furnished cabin of a magnificent pleasure boat and up onto the deck where a wonderful panorama was revealed: a perfect, bright summer's night with a gleaming, star-filled sky and a brilliantly lit city, which shimmered on the horizon; then the city faded away into the distance, the night cleared and the scene took us to a barren heath, which soon gave way to a desolate cemetery.

Once again, there was a break in the landscape before the final series of sets: a bedroom, without many pieces of furniture, then a lounge with a round table and a carved sideboard, a café terrace in an Islamic country with waiters wearing fezzes and short red waistcoats, embroidered with gold thread, the interior of a Parisian café and finally a large public park at the bottom of the Champs Elysées, with English nannies and child-nurses from Alsace, fashionable women in calashes, a small puppet theatre and a blue-and-orange canvas-covered roundabout with its horses and their stylised manes and its two gondolas decorated with a large orange sun.

The notice in the catalogue described how this miniature panorama had been found in France, by Hermann Raffke himself, in a junkshop in the Belleville quarter of Paris. The collector had been particularly taken with the somewhat enigmatic nature of the sets it represented and had had a considerable amount of research done in an attempt to discover what melodrama they referred to. The most likely hypothesis had been that they were a series of sets for one of those long "animated charades" which were all the rage in Parisian salons around the 1880s. But nobody had been able to give him any more precise information.

The starting price which the Raffke heirs insisted on – $2,500 – caused a stir in the sales room. Despite the high quality of the drawings and their fine colours, the work was unsigned, belonged more to the realm of toys, or of knick-knacks at the most, than to the world of art, and it had almost no market value. But doubtlessly the strange, almost disconcerting charm given off by the work, which had immediately attracted Hermann Raffke, began finally to work on the buyers. For, after dropping as low as $400, the bidding picked up rapidly, finally stopping at $6,000.

The second European painting was a work by Hogarth entitled *The Upside-Down Manor* (No. 83 in the catalogue). The painter had reworked a theme he had tackled several times in his series of so-called "didactic" engravings, where the intention was to show how putting the perspective slightly out of true can sometimes create strange illusions: an ostler feeds a horse which is standing a long way away from him, for example, or a person standing on a first-floor balcony shakes hands with someone on the ground floor, and so on. Here, such phenomena had occurred in the main sitting-room of a Gothic-style manor: a footman lights a candle which is situated at the other side of the room, another serves a drink to a gentleman who is sitting way above him, and a woman at the top of the staircase presents her hand to be kissed to a man standing at its bottom.

In this case, the prestige of the signature and the strange-

149

ness of the subject were plainly worth more than the painting itself, which was rather clumsily done, uncertain in its effects, with dull colours and in a very poor state of conservation. In fact it was more reminiscent of an amusing innsign than of a masterwork. But this did not stop its rapidly breaking through the $10,000 mark.

The only thing European about the third painting (No. 93) was its artist. It was a *Tennessee Landscape* painted by a Frenchman, Auguste Hervieu, during his stay in the United States as a young painter between 1827 and 1831. Born in Paris in 1794, but brought up in England where he worked under the guidance of Sir Thomas Lawrence, Auguste Hervieu accompanied Mrs Frances Trollope, the famous novelist's mother, when she tried to make her fortune in America. For some time, Hervieu was an art teacher in a Utopian colony which Mrs Wright, a friend of Mrs Trollope, had set up in Nashoba, near Memphis, and the picture in the Raffke Collection dated from this period. He later moved to Cincinnati before going back to France, where he seems to have given up painting. At the time of the first Raffke Sale, Auguste Hervieu's entire known output consisted of only thirty lithographs (used to illustrate Frances Trollope's pamphlet, *Domestic Manners of the Americans*), eleven watercolours, three sketch books and four canvases. Half a dozen fanatical collectors fought one another ferociously over them and this pleasant, though rather affected landscape, which the experts valued at only five or six hundred dollars, reached a record selling price of $7,500 after a fierce struggle between Stephen Siriel, the agent for the film star Anastasia Swanson, who was then at the peak of her fame, and the industrialist K. P. Inverness, president and managing director of the Altiplano Railroad Company.

* * *

It is difficult to know exactly what the Raffke heirs' intentions were at the end of this sale. On the evening of the last day, cards were handed round announcing that a second sale, mainly devoted to old European works, would take place as soon as they had solved the many, complex problems posed by drawing up the catalogue, the initial drafting of which had been entrusted to Messrs William Fleish, Professor of the History of Art at Carson College, New York, and Gregory Feuerabends, chief auctioneer at Parke and Bernett's and purchasing advisor to the Museum of Fine Arts in Philadelphia.

In fact, several years were to pass by. The First World War broke out and the Raffke heirs probably thought it wiser to lie low while American public opinion was showing distinctly anti-German tendencies, especially in towns where the German community was large and well organized. After the explosion of the munitions depot on Black Tom Island, which was attributed to German spies, there were demonstrations on the streets of Cleveland, Milwaukee, Chicago and Pittsburgh and, in this last town, some of the Raffke Brewery's windows were smashed. Then, when the United Stated entered the war, one thousand eight hundred German citizens suspected of Pan-Germanic activities were interned on Ellis Island, including the deputy editor of the Pittsburgh *Vaterland*. Anything more or less reminiscent of the huge Germanophile festivities of 1913 would only have provoked public, if not governmental, hostility.

The second Raffke Sale took place only in 1924. Meanwhile, the Raffke heirs, who had had the prescience to foresee the Volstead amendment, had transferred their brewery to Canada. What is more, two books had come out which contained a considerable amount of new information concerning the brewer's collection, some of which, at least in the art world and market, was positively revolutionary.

The first of these books was Hermann Raffke's autobiography, written up by two of his sons from drafts and notebooks discovered after his death, and published by Moffat and Yard, New York, in 1921. In a frequently pompous and turgid style, the brewer began by evoking the vague memories he had of his place of birth, Travenmunde, a small village near Lübeck, where his father worked as a horse dealer. He then told how he was apprenticed at the age of twelve to a cooper in Hamburg, whose workshop looked out over the harbour, where he would spend hours daydreaming about the large sailing-ships which had come from the four corners of the earth, loaded with rare woods, silk and other strange commodities. At the age of sixteen he took ship as a carpenter aboard a Danish whaler, the *Philoctetes*, which was wrecked off Iceland. Rescued by some Newfoundland fishermen, he finished up in Portland, Maine, where he was employed to work on the Great Lakes. From then, his life story was that of a typical self-made man: starting out as a waiter on a paddle-steamer on Lake Michigan earning a dollar and a half per week, he then became proprietor of a soda-fountain by the Niagara Falls, got a concession to sell refreshments at the Kalamazoo dogtrack, then the sole distribution rights on beers, sodas and spirits to the seventeen largest eateries in Chicago, before setting up a brewery with three associates, whom he rapidly eliminated, which was to become the biggest in the town, and soon in the state.

By 1875, at the age of forty-five, he had amassed almost ten million dollars and his two eldest sons were now old enough to replace him. While gradually handing over control of the business to them, he decided to concentrate entirely on his collection of paintings.

This liking for art had started when he had been working by the Niagara Falls. He had furnished a small room in the attic of his soda-fountain and used to rent it out at a quarter per night to artists who had come to paint the Falls. One of them, who had stayed almost a month, gave him in lieu of payment a picture called *Whisky Drinkers:* it depicted a smoky bar in a small fishing port; through the dirty yellow panes of the window a misty landscape could be made out, with a few boats and a line of sailors in sou'-westers pulling their nets onto the beach; inside the bar, three rough-looking men were sitting round a table of undressed timber in front of three thick glass tumblers and a dark, wide-bellied bottle.

Raffke had hung this painting behind his bar. He fully realized that it was not very well drawn, that the men did not really look as though they were sitting on their stools, that their arms were too short and the whole thing lacked colour. But he felt happy whenever he looked at his painting and used to tell himself that one day, when he was rich, he would have lots more.

Three years later, when he got married and settled in Kalamazoo, he bought another four. The first two were chosen by his wife at a charity auction and depicted respectively: *Two Small Cats Asleep* and a *Group of Quakeresses in the Port of Nantucket.* The third was called *Tiger Hunting* and showed an elephant, carrying a howdah, struggling with a big cat which it had seized in its trunk. The howdah has been turned half over in the struggle, throwing to the ground a waif-like mahout dressed only in a piece of cloth wrapped round his loins, a glabrous European with thick red sideburns armed with a long carbine, and a maharajah wearing a richly embroidered, jewel-studded costume; at either side of the elephant, the apparently terrified natives have thrown themselves to the ground.

The fourth painting was called *Café Waiters*. It depicted three waiters in tailcoats lined up in front of a gleaming copper bar counter, each carrying a silver tray bearing, respectively, a lobster, an almost perfectly translucent flan, and an extravagant set-piece decked with peacock feathers. Tall mirrors had been placed above the bar, behind the rows of bottles, in which the restaurant was reflected with its gold, stucco, mouldings, large chandeliers, its over-elaborate desserts and its glittering clientele in dress-coats, crinoline ballgowns and bemedalled uniforms.

This was his favourite, for it reminded him of his early career and it went perfectly with the *Whisky Drinkers*. He hung them side-by-side in the tiny dining room of the two-room flat where he and his wife had just set up home.

During the years that followed, Hermann Raffke had little time to enlarge his collection. In 1875 he had, in all, just twenty-three paintings. But he would henceforth have both the time and money necessary to satisfy his long-suppressed passion.

The last sixty pages of the book contained the most interesting revelations concerning his collection. They consisted of a succinct, but detailed account of the eleven trips Hermann Raffke had made to Europe between 1875 and 1909. No attempt had been made to write up these notes and reading them soon became tiresome as, page after page, they went through the brewer's daily business: visits to studios and galleries, consultations with experts, contacts with agents, lunches with artists and dealers, meetings with collectors, restorers, frame-makers, forwarding-agents, bankers and so on. His two sons had not hesitated in publishing entire pages from his diaries and logbooks, even including railway timetables, his daily bookkeeping and mentions of, for example, the purchasing of some razorblades or having twelve cambric shirts made at Doucet's. They had simply added on a few explanatory notes, either from their father's letters in which he told of his movements, his acquisitions and, always briefly, of his impressions; or else from conversations they had had with him on his return. Various documents were also appended; for example, sales catalogues in which the collector had ticked the numbers that interested him.

Hermann Raffke was quite aware that he did not know much about paintings, be they old or modern. His personal taste would have naturally led him to buy large historical canvases or *genre* paintings telling comforting anecdotes. But he distrusted his personal taste, particularly when it came to building up a collection that would make the Tompkins and the Dillmans of the world turn green with jealousy, and he decided to get advice. Of the two hundred and fifty or so paintings which he brought back from Europe, only twenty – which he called his "Lieblingssünde", that is to say, his little peccadillos – were directly purchased by him and corresponded to his hidden tastes.* All the others were

---

* Seven of them meant so much to him chat he asked Kürz to include them in his *Gallery Portrait*: Julien Blévy's *Concini's Murder*, a grandiose construction marred by an excessive use of bitumen; *The Field of the Cloth of Gold*, by Guillaume Rorret, who was called, even by himself, a "Post-Raphaelite"; *The Death of the Maid Servant*, by Henry Silverspoon, best known for his decoration of the smoking-room in the Crystal Palace; *Tilling in Norway*, by a Dane, Dolknif Schlamperer (the son of a sailor who had perished in the wreck of the *Philoctetes* and Raffke granted him a life pension in memory of his father); Camille Velin-Ravel's *Launcelot*, a large, cold composition in which this pupil of Couture and friend of Puvis de Chavannes has shown the Knight of the Charet after nightfall entering the giant Meliagaunt's castle, where Guinevere is being held prisoner; *The Masked Prince*, by the Tyrolean painter Horvendill Lauten-

acquired through his advisors. "The most eminent critics, the most scrupulous experts and the most cautious art historians will be responsible for my collection and be its guarantors, thanks to them it will be one of the most beautiful in the whole of the United States of America," so he wrote to his wife in 1875 while sailing back across the Atlantic for the first time, aboard the S.S. *Kaiser Wilhelm der Grosse*. And it seems that he really did follow their advice blindly. Thus, at the Vianello Sale of September 17th 1895, at the Palazzo Sarezin, he bid as high as two hundred thousand francs[†] for a *St John the Baptist* by Groziano, before letting it go to his rival ("a big lump of a Frenchwoman accompanied by an overdressed brat", he noted in the margin of his catalogue) simply because the expert that was with him, Professor Aldenhoven, head curator of the Wallraff-Richartz Museum of Cologne, had told him that no American collector owned one of this painter's works. And he only gave up when Aldenhoven finally pleaded with him to.

Some thirty advisors accordingly guided Hermann Raffke's choices. The most highly reputed among them were undoubtedly Gottlieb Heringsdorf, who was at that time putting together his monumental *History of Italian Art* and who accompanied the brewer on three occasions to Turin and to Milan, Emilio Zannoni, curator of the Museum of Florence, Busching the Berlin art-dealer, and the American critic Thomas Greenback, whose monograph on the

---

macher, a mediocre pupil of Charles Haeberlin at the Stuttgart academy; and *La Première Ascension du Mont Cervin*, by the Swiss painter Gustave Feuerstahl, which portrays in melodramatic realism the terrible fall of Hadow, Hudson, Lord Douglas and Michel Croz, and the miraculous escape of Edward Whymper and the Taugwalder brothers.

† Italy being at that time part of the *Union Latine*, the franc was legal tender. (Author's note)

Carracci family first demonstrated the key role played by Ludovico. Others, such as Maxfield Parrish, Frantz Ingehalt or Albert Arnkle, were young art teachers at the time and only proved their competence many years later; others still were merely what might be called well-informed amateurs and if they did become famous later, this was never thanks to their art criticism: for instance, Alfred Blumenstich, who travelled with Raffke in Bavaria long before he became a banker; or Lawrence Inglesby, First Secretary at the United States Embassy in Berne; or Theodor Fontane, who was not yet the popular novelist he was to become in the 1880s; or Joshua Ewett, whom Raffke met in Venice while the young architect was working on the restoration of Santa Maria degli Zvevi, and who tells in his memoirs how the idea of setting up the chain of hotels, which many years later was to make him a wealthy man, first came to him while cruising around the Mediterranean with the brewer.

Most of these advisors were German or American, perhaps from xenophobia or jingoism, but most probably because of the language barrier; indeed, they did feature a few Englishmen (including John Sparkes, who drew up the excellent catalogue of the Dulwich College collection of paintings), three Swiss (Reinhardt Burckhardt, curator of the Museum of Basle, not to be confused with his distant cousin Jakob, the art historian and friend of Nietzsche; Lengacker, the painter from Berne; and Anton Pfann, the Zurich art-dealer), but only two Italians (Zannoni and Franco Veglioni, the editor of the *Befana* review), one Dutchman (Ernst Moes, head of the Rijks Museum's collection of prints) and one Frenchman (Henri Pontier, at the time a lecturer at the University of Aix, but who was to become a highly successful comic trooper under the stagename "La Flanelle" – the tendency to round French songs off with a "tagada tsoin tsoin" apparently goes back to him, though this has today become a highly debatable point).

One thing at least is certain and that is that Hermann Raffke was generally satisfied with the advice he was given. It only very rarely gave him cause for complaint. In a letter to his eldest son, Michael, dated September 4th 1900 and postmarked Paris, where he had been invited to visit the Exposition by Jeremy Woodward, General Commissioner of the United States Section, he considered that he had made a mistake in allowing himself to be talked into buying two modern paintings (Bonnard's *La Rue d'Aveyron* and Renoir's *Cigarette Salesgirl*) for twenty-five thousand francs, which Busching had absolutely insisted on his purchasing; *not that they are unattractive*, he added, *even though I do not much care for this kind of painting, but I am sure that I could have paid three times less for them, even bearing in mind the rather exorbitant prices being asked in Paris this year.* And in another letter, postmarked Munich, May 1904, he told his nephew Humbert, to whom he had entrusted his collection in Pittsburgh, that he was putting back on the market three pictures by Menzel (*St Wendel Station, Level-Crossing near Kissingen* and *The Artist's Studio*) which he had bought a week before on Blumenstich's advice. But these are the only examples of any disagreement. What most often happened was that the brewer was so confident in his purchases that his advisors had to restrain, rather than encourage him. For example, just before the great Barrattini Sale in Rome in 1888, Zannoni wrote him a long letter (reproduced in its entirety in the book) putting him on guard against being prematurely over-enthusiastic:

> . . . I have had the opportunity to take a closer look at those works which everyone has been saying will be

this auction's revelations, and I must say that this has done nothing to calm those justified suspicions which a mere perusal of the catalogue had raised in me. Le Donnaiolo's *Portrait of Cardinal Barberini* is in a very poor state of conservation and, in any case, this painter is quite unworthy of the praises that it has been considered fashionable to heap on him for the last twenty-odd years. I also found the two Bellagambas disappointing: no doubt, his *Adoration of the Shepherds* does have its qualities, although the positioning of the characters has simply been lifted from Perugino and the distribution of light is altogether dull; but I found his *Conversion of St Paul* far below the reputation which Cannochiali has made for it: the canvas has been worked over so much since it was saved from the fire in Saint-Paul-outside-the-Walls that all it has left of Bellagamba is his name. If that! For I am personally convinced that it is not by Cristofano, but by his son, Domenico. As for *Hercules at Omphale's Feet*, which they are trying to pass off as a Guido Reni, it is a workshop production and I would not give more than six hundred francs for it. But you'll see. It will fetch at least thirty thousand. Keep well away from the bidding and do not allow yourself to be taken in by prestigious signatures which conceal what are, in my opinion, minor works. On the other hand, I cannot advise you too strongly to take a close interest in three paintings whose worth seems to me to be indisputable. They are signed by relatively little-known artists, but their reputations are beginning to become firmly established and you can be certain that their market value will continue to rise.

The first one is No. 37: *Sleeping Musicians*, by

Arrigo Mattei, one of Crespi's finest pupils and, in his use of chiaroscuro, in no way inferior to his master (on the other hand, be on your guard concerning *Dice Players* (No. 37b) which, I have good reason to believe, has been misattributed to him. This has now become a typical ploy in public auctions: given that two canvases have the same format and frame, the heirs try to pass them off as a pair, and they are certainly going to try to sell them as one lot; but there is no reason why you should allow yourself to be taken in.)

The second painting I should like to recommend is No. 52: *The Sack of Troy*, by Otto Reder, oil on canvased paper. This was originally a projected stageset for the prologue of Racquet's *Aeneas* at the Lisbon Opera. You no doubt know that Reder had just been appointed its official scene-painter when he was killed in the terrible earthquake of 1755. The work has been restored, but extremely sensitively, by his pupil Moraes-Salgado. I know that you already possess several conflagrations, especially the Van den Eeckhout, but I am convinced that this one will give you complete satisfaction.

The third painting, No. 78, should be especially close to your heart, as it concerns two of your compatriots: it is the *Portrait of Wilhelm von Humholdt*, painted by Peter von Cornelius in 1806. Humboldt was at that time the Prussian *chargé d'affaires* in Rome, where Cornelius was working on the decoration of the Barrattini Palace. I do not have much time for Cornelius's neo-classicism, which I always find a little "fake", but I must say that this portrait is splendid. I should also point out that this is the only portrait known to be by him. You will certainly be bidding against Strudellhoff, for I learnt last night at a *soirée* given by la Schwanzleben that he has been given the job of getting the painting back for the Embassy. But he will definitely not go higher than one thousand five hundred or two thousand dollars. This work belongs in your collection. It will make a perfect match with the Bassano which I had you buy five years ago and with the little Princess which that great tomfool of a Veglioni sold you . . . etc.

Raffke followed Zannoni's instructions to the letter. He demanded that the two Matteis be put on auction separately, and got his way; he let the buyers fight over the Guido Reni, the Donnaiolo and the two Bellagambas, each of them fetching more than two hundred thousand francs, while he acquired his three paintings for less than one hundred thousand. Today, they feature in Heinrich Kürz's *A Gallery Portrait*, among the hundred finest works in his collection, which he lists entirely in the last pages of his book, giving for each of them the date and circumstances of its acquisition, and sometimes even the price paid. We shall limit ourselves to citing just the first few, those which he describes as follows: "These fifteen paintings are the fifteen jewels in the crown of this German by birth, American at heart and collector by calling, and which I am proudest of having brought together."

Dutch School: *Portrait of a Young Girl "With Harbour Chart"*, also called the *Cuijper Portrait*, since it was long part of the collection of the Belgian art historian Emil Cuijper. Generally attributed to Carel Fabritius of Delft. Purchased in March, 1896 in Berlin from the art-dealer Adolf Kieseritzky.

Hans Holbein the Younger: *Portrait of the Merchant Martin Baumgarten*. After having travelled through Egypt, Arabia and Syria at the beginning of the sixteenth century, Baumgarten settled in Cologne where he worked for the Imstenraedt brothers. From 1529 to 1536, he managed the brothers' counter at the Stalhof in London. This is one of the first portraits that Holbein painted in England, since it dates to the very year of his arrival in London (1532). Purchased in London in 1909 (Wyndham Sale).

Flemish School: *The Siege of Tyre*. In front of the castellated walls of a burning town, hundreds of men drag enormous platforms carrying narrow columns full of archers, *catapulta* and military machines. The sky is criss-crossed with flaming brands. Spectacular fire-effects empurple the horizon. Purchased in Saint-Gall in 1901 (details of the sale not specified).

Gaspard Ten Broek: *A Picardy Landscape*. Purchased from an antiques dealer in the rue de Lille in 1875.

Italian School: *Portrait of a Knight*, also called *The Knight of the Bath*. Purchased in Venice in October, 1896, from Count Fadengelb. At the beginning of the nineteenth century, this painting belonged to the Sostegno family of Turin, who sold it to Redern, the Berlin art collector, who passed it on to Prince Lichnowsky, at whose death Count Fadengelb inherited it. The naked knight is seen from the back, standing in front of a spring where he is about to bathe, and which sends back a perfect reflection of his naked body, seen face on. To the right of the picture, a burnished steel breast-plate leans against a dead tree trunk, reflecting the knight's right profile in every detail, while, on the other side, a woman dressed in long flowing robes holds out a large round shield, which reflects his left profile, just slightly distorted by the shield's gleaming convexity. Who painted this picture, the formal perfection of which gives off an almost unbearable feeling of serenity, has been the subject of heated debate. It is generally attributed to a painter of the Brescia School, perhaps Girolamo Romanino, or Moretta da Brescia, or Girolamo Savoldo il Bresciano. But some critics favour a painter from Ferrara.

Italian School: *The Annunciation by the Rocks.* In the midst of a precipitous, jagged landscape, a sort of grotto has been formed where the Virgin sits with an open book on her lap. She does not seem to have noticed the Archangel Gabriel who, a few paces away, leans towards her with a lily in his hand. In the distance some hunters and their pack pursue a stag. Previously belonged to the collection of Doctor Heideking of Hamburg. Purchased in 1891 for two thousand marks through James Tienappel, the wine merchant.

Chardin: *Luncheon Preparations.* Bears signature and date on the edge of the stone table: J. S. Chardin 17(32?). Purchased for six thousand five hundred francs on May 9th 1881, at the Beurnonville Sale. Baron Beurnonville, who had acquired it from Laurent Laperlier, used to call it *The Pink Meal*, because of all the shades of pink in the food it depicted (salmon, vineyard peaches, ham, and so on).

Gerbrand van den Eeckhout: *Enée Fuyant les Ruines de Troie.* A large composition of the same subject has been conserved in Munich. This one, on a much smaller scale (80 x 50 cm), concentrates more on the conflagration of the town than on the characters. Under a stormy crepuscular sky, lit up by the gleam of the conflagration, stand the smoking ruins of Troy; in their midst, the great disembowelled Horse looks like a mythical beast. Aeneas and Anchises are mere off-white figures fleeing in the distance (details of the acquisition not specified).

Lucas Cranach: *Portrait of Jakob Ziegler.* Discovered in the cellars of the Zum Sängerhaus Brewery in Strasburg, this work was studied and authenticated by Professor Jérôme Adrien. It was in Wittenberg that the painter happened to encounter Ziegler, who had come to visit Luther before returning to Strasburg, where his *Theatrum Orbis Terrarum* appeared in 1532. Purchased in Zurich from Anton Pfann in 1901.

Dutch School: *Young Girl Reading a Letter.* Purchased in Brussels in 1904 from the widow of Stallaert, the painter of historical subjects. The main interest of this little composition is the way in which the light is made to enter the room, where a girl stands by a high narrow window, which is just ajar. Stallaert thought that it was a juvenile work by Metsu, but this attribution cannot be accepted for lack of documentary evidence.

School of Pisanello (?): *Portrait of a Princess of the House of Este.* The painting was rediscovered in 1877 by Veglioni in the shop of a Milanese pawnbroker, who claimed that he did not know where it had come from. Veglioni showed it to Viscount Tauzia, who recognized it as being one of the paintings stolen, eight years previously, from Doctor Bernasconi of Verona (whose splendid collection was soon to form the basis of the town's museum). Bernasconi held it to be a genuine Pisanello, but Tauzia showed that this was impossible:

the princess in question (Lauredana d'Este, the future wife of Aimeri de Gonzague) being only three years old when the painter died.

Italian School: *The Visitation*. One of the few European paintings purchased in the United States (Boston, Sherwood Sale, February 1900) where it was put on auction as "attributed to Paris Bordone". An expertise was carried out by Thomas Greenback, who pointed out that the livery of the page-boys bears the arms of Cardinal d'Amboise and therefore the painter could only be Andrea Solario, whom Chaumont d'Amboise had summoned to France to decorate the chapel of his château in Gaillon (unfortunately destroyed in 1793).

Leandro Bassano: *Portrait of an Ambassador*. Identified as Angelo da Campari, Envoy Plenipotentiary of the Republic of Venice to Abbas the Great, Shah of Persia, then to Gustavus Adolphus, King of Sweden. Purchased in Rome in 1883 for four thousand francs from the last descendant of the subject, the poet Gianbattista Doganieri.

Jan Vermeer of Delft: *The Stolen Epistle*. Ruskin's description of it made it famous and, more than any other work, it doubtlessly contributed to the painter's reinstatement. Purchased in 1875 for thirty guineas from William Jensen, the London merchant, who presented it as being a "Van der Meer of Haarlem, pupil of Berghem", it had previously belonged to the collection of Simon Frehude, the archaeologist.

Degas: *Dancers*. Purchased from the artist in January 1896 for sixty thousand francs. The meeting between the painter and the collector was arranged by Mr Gawdy, the United

States Consul in Paris. Messrs Gawdy and Raffke arrived at 37, rue Victor-Macé at about eleven o'clock in the morning, saw round the studio, then took Degas out to eat some Colchester oysters at the Maison Dorée.

The second work, published in 1923 by Bennington University Press, was a thesis devoted to Heinrich Kürz's oeuvre: *Heinrich Kürz, An American Artist, 1884–1914*. It was written by none other than Lester Nowak. While working on his article for the *Bulletin of the Ohio School of Arts*, Nowak had met Kürz and the two of them had become friends. After the artist's tragic death (he was one of the twenty-three victims of the Long Island train crash on August 12th 1914), his sister asked Nowak to help her sort out the countless notes, sketches, roughs and preparatory studies which she had found in his studio, and to draw up a *catalogue raisonné*. This catalogue, along with a considerable *apparatus criticus*, made up the bulk of his thesis since, as he put it in his brief foreword, the author had refrained "from any sort of aesthetic judgement in order to concentrate on the technical problems related to an *oeuvre* which, in its very brevity, has something unique and exemplary about it".

Death had not cut short Heinrich Kürz's career. He had stopped painting of his own accord at the end of 1912, after completing *A Gallery Portrait*, which Hermann Raffke had commissioned from him and which it had taken him almost three and a half years to paint. In fact, his entire *œuvre* consists of only six canvases: two *Seafront Scenes*, painted while he was on holiday in Watermill in July 1901; the *Portrait of Miss Fanny Bentham in the Role of Camille in "On ne Badine pas avec l'Amour"*, at Pittsburgh's central theatre; an *Anamorphic Self-Portrait*, left unfinished; a *genre* painting, entitled *Central Pacific*, depicting Red Indians on horseback watching a large locomotive pass by; and *A Gallery Portrait*. But for this one painting there were no fewer than 1,397 drawings, roughs and assorted sketches, and Lester Nowak needed almost three hundred pages in order to analyse this prodigious quantity of material.

Nowak had obviously not been able to see the painting itself again, since it had been inhumed for ever with its owner, and the only reproduction of the whole that he could provide came from a mediocre photograph, surreptitiously taken by one of the guards of the room where the painting had been exhibited. The publication of several sketches in which Kürz had set out the positions of the model, the easel, the dog, the arrangement of the main paintings and the painting itself "in infinite regression" allowed an almost complete reconstruction of the work to be made, while at the same time highlighting its difficult gestation, as though the positioning of the different elements and the way they worked respectively, and interactively, had only crystallized in the artist's mind after patient mental labour. For example, in the early sketches the gallery was depicted with much more verism: an enormous room with doors and windows opening out onto a terrace decorated with potted trees; a large Venetian chandelier; some pieces of furniture; display cases containing various knick-knacks and curios (nautiluses, armillary spheres, a theorbo and a mandolin, a stuffed parrot); some ten people and only a few paintings. It was only as the sketches developed that the scene became visibly more concentrated, more rarefied, more dense and compact, until nothing was admitted except "the paintings themselves, their master and their reflections".

It should however be borne in mind that Raffke had initially asked Kürz to depict him with all of his family, that is to say with his wife, his five sons, his daughter, his three daughters-in-law, his son-in-law, his seven grandchildren and his nephew Humbert (whom he had adopted after his brother's death). When Kürz decided to include just one human being in front of the collection of paintings, he thought up a way of respecting the brewer's wishes by transforming certain copies of portraits in the collection into portraits of members of the Raffke family: thus, a fairly idealized Mrs Raffke replaces the *Portrait of Clara Schumann* by Ludwig Steinbruck; the five sons (the eldest with his magnificent black beard, the youngest, born one-eyed, with a black eye-bandage) and his son-in-law feature in a version of James Ensor's *Self-Portrait With Masks* (close, in its inspiration, to the one in the Lambotte Collection), purchased in Brussels in 1904 at the "Libre Esthétique" Exhibition at Albert Arnkle's insistence; Anna, the brewer's only daughter, is depicted in the features of Fabritius's *Young Girl with Harbour Chart*: the three daughters-in-law are the *Three Fates* by an anonymous Italian of the sixteenth century; the seven grandchildren appear in a painting by Boucher, called *The Riddle*; and the robust *Mephistopheles* by Larry Gibson (American School) gives way to a placid Humbert Raffke, whose small twinkling eyes are screwed up in delight behind his steel-rimmed spectacles.

But the main interest of the thesis lay elsewhere. By publishing for the first time Kürz's preparatory sketches side-by-side with the originals from the Raffke Collection (exceptional permission to reproduce them having been granted by the heirs), Nowak finally solved the riddle of those tiny variations which had so intrigued visitors to the exhibition:

This is not, as I suggested ten years ago in my first

appraisal of the work, an ironic procedure aimed at reinstating that certainly attractive, but self-regarding, idea of the "freedom of the artist" when confronted with the world which he has been commercially commissioned to reproduce; nor is it a historico-critical perspective, allotting to the artist the unbearable inheritance of some vague "Golden Age" or "Paradise Lost"; on the contrary, it is a process of incorporation, of acquisition: a simultaneous projection towards the Other, and Theft, in the Promethean sense of the term. This psychological, rather than aesthetic, procedure is surely sufficiently aware of its own limitations to be able to turn itself, when necessary, into derision and denounce itself as an illusion, as a mere exacerbation of that form of perception which can produce only *trompe l'oeil*; but above all, we should see in it the logical end of the purely mental construct which exactly defines the work of the artist: the fragile borders which constitute the narrow field of all artistic creation have been drawn between Correggio's *Anch'io son' Pittore* and Poussin's *J'apprends à regarder*, and the final result of this can only be Silence, that self-willed and self-destructive silence which Kürz imposed on himself after finishing this work.

The demonstration of this theory was accompanied by an exceptionally erudite study of the paintings in the Raffke Collection, as though Nowak were anxious to convince his readers that what was at stake in *A Gallery Portrait* had as much to do with the original works, as it had with Heinrich Kürz's slightly falsified reworkings of them. Thanks to the kindness of Humbert Raffke, who had continued to take care of the collection since his uncle's death, Nowak had been given access to all the documents concerning the brewer's European acquisitions and had, with astonishing patience, ingenuity and flair, been able to reconstruct the history of nearly all of the paintings and quite often to make specific attributions. So it was that he had been able to confrm Greenback's hypothesis concerning Andrea Solario's *Visitation* by establishing a complete list of its owners from Cardinal d'Amboise to James Sherwood: presented by the Cardinal to Maximilian, during the setting up of the League of Cambrai, the *Visitation* by Del Gobbo (even though it was his brother, Cristoforo, who was the hunchback, Andrea was still nicknamed "Del Gobbo") was to remain for almost a century in the collections of Charles V, then of Philip II who, when Albert the Pious married his daughter, gave it to his new son-in-law. The painting then entered the collection of Charles de Croy, Duke of Arschot, doubtlessly by way of Geneviève d'Urfé, Marquise de Croy and Isabelle's lady-in-waiting. It is thus mentioned in the inventory which the painter Salomon Noveliers drew up after the Duke's death, as well as in the public announcement when this remarkable collection was put on auction:

> Let it hereby be known that among the chattels-personal of the late regretted Lord Duke of Arschot are to be numbered circa two thousand pictorial items of every sort of colour and from the hands of divers masters, viz: Albrecht Dürer, Lucas van Leyden, Mabuse, Hieronymus Bosch, Florus Dayck, Pieter Aertsen, Titian Urban, Andrea del Gobbo, Paolo Veronese et cetera. Circa eighteen thousand medallions, a library of six thousand tomes, many of the afore-said being manuscripts, much plain as well as gilded silverware,

vases of rock-crystal and of ophite, agates, amber, jasper, bloodstones and many another crafted gem, rareties of every sort, arrases. Such indeed a wealth of fine chattels that scarce could the like be found in any Prince's Palace; of which chattels the Public Sale shall take place, under the ordinance of the Devisees and Executors of the said Lord Duke's Last Will and Testament, in the city of Brussels on the fifteenth day of this month of July, to the last and highest bidder, and shall proceed until the completion of the afore-said.

At this auction, which took place in Antwerp not Brussels, the painting was purchased by a merchant, Jan Wildens, who had two small copies of it made by Erasmus Quellyn, one of which was sent to London and the other to Vienna (one of these copies is today part of the Princess Charlotte Collection in the Miramar Palace, near Trieste), before passing it on to Boyer d'Arguille, a counsellor to the Parliament of Provence, for sixty florins; this sale took place by way of Coelmans, whom Boyer d'Arguille had summoned to Aix to make engravings of his collection of paintings, and the one he made of the Solario is today still preserved in the Museum of Aix-en-Provence's collection of prints and engravings. The painting's presence in the chapel of Château d'Arguille is attested until 1790. During the revolution, it vanished and, in 1824, was rediscovered in a wine merchant's house in Moncoutant by a notary from Loches, Charles Maurepas, who published a fine description of it in the *Bulletin des Sociétés Savantes d'Indre-et-Loire* (1828, XVII, 43) but misattributed it to Paris Bordone. In 1851, the work was put on auction in Angoulême (Coignières Sale, no. 1 in the catalogue: *The Visitation*, Italian School, 16th Century. Attributed to Paris Bordone) and was acquired for two hundred francs by a local antiques dealer, who was to take it with him to the United States in 1885 and sell it to James Sherwood that very same year.

Similarly precise information was also given concerning Devéria's *The Ummayed Mosque*, the *Loing at Montargis*, which Nowak authenticated as one of Girodet's rare landscapes, the *Arabian Knights*, his attribution of it to Delacroix being based on an impeccable bibliography, and the particularly unusual *Interior with Wig* (beside a heavy armchair of gilded wood, with Beauvais upholstery, stands an occasional table on which a tricorne decked with a black plume lies next to a massive blond wig, perched on a sculpted wooden head) which Nowak peremptorily identified as the "shop-sign" which Binet, wigmaker to King Louis XIV, commissioned from Rigaud in 1681, of which the existence had been suspected from a mediocre epigram attributed to Bachaumont:

> Binet, wigmaker to the King,
> Asked Rigaud to paint him a sign.
> But Rigaud is vexed with this thing,
> For combs push his brush out of line.
> Yet, Rigaud, if your own models
> Lacked the wigs they wear when you paint
> None could tell your *bows* from your bells,
> And you'd have true cause for complaint!

The two major revelations of this study concerned the *Annunciation by the Rocks* and the *Knight of the Bath*. Basing his argument on the large number of similarities between the Annunciation and certain details of the *Vision of St Eustace* in the National Gallery (the stag, the mottled dog, the little greyhound), of the *Legend of St George* in

Santa Anastasia (the two dogs beside St George) and of the *Annunciation* in San Fermo of Verona (the angel's wings and the cut of the landscape above him), Nowak showed that this painting could indeed, without reasonable doubt, be attributed to Pisanello.

As for the *Knight of the Bath*, Nowak brilliantly linked it with a lost work by Giorgione, described in Vasari's *Lives*:

> In order to convince the sculptors that his art was superior to theirs, he (Giorgione) said that he would show them the back, the front and the two sides in profile of one single countenance in a painting; which put them all to confusion. This is how he proceeded: he positioned a naked man, seen from behind, who had a spring of limpid water on the ground in front of him, in which Giorgione painted the naked man's facial reflection; on one side, there was a small breast-plate, in which appeared his left profile, for every detail could be discerned in its polished metal; on the other side was a mirror reflecting the naked man's other profile. This was something of marvellous invention and fancy which indeed demonstrated that painting demands more talent and labour and can show more of nature in one regard than sculpture. . .

This same play with reflecting surfaces could also be found in another lost work, a *St George* described by Paolo Pino. But no other precise attestation of these works existed and, what is more, several painters in Venice, Ferrara and Brescia had used similar procedures to varying effect (in particular Savoldo's *Full-Length Portrait, said to be of Gaston de Foix*, now in the Louvre). But it was during his attempt to discover how it had become part of the Sostegno Collection that Nowak had made his major discovery, which was to allow him to affirm that this work was indeed by Giorgione. He had in fact found traces of a painting the description of which tallied exactly with the *Knight of the Bath* in the Sostegno Collection. This painting, entitled *Venus Giving the Arms of Vulcan to Aeneas*, had been left in the will of a certain Nicolo Renieri and had been put on sale in Venice at the beginning of the seventeenth century. Now, another painting from the same inheritance – "a small picture with two figures from the hand of Zorzo of Castelfranco" – was attested in Gabriele Vendramin's *Camerino delle Antigaglie* of 1567. This *Venus* certainly did not figure in the catalogue of this collector, who had owned several Giorgiones (including *The Tempest*, the *Dead Christ Borne up by an Angel* and the little *Flute Player*, now in the Borghese Gallery), nor was it mentioned in Marcantonio Michiel's invaluable descriptions of the collection, but the coincidence of Vasari's description with the painting's having belonged to a group of works partly or completely inherited from a well-known collector of Giorgiones was too strong a clue not to allow a possible attribution, which no iconographic or aesthetic argument could contradict.

American painting takes only a small place in Lester Nowak's study. Of the twenty-one pictures of American origin that are depicted in the *Gallery Portrait*, only five are dealt with in any depth. The first three are of historical subjects, in which the theme, documentary interest and the characters portrayed count for far more than artistic worth, or their artists' fame. The first is called *Charles Wilkes Arriving in San Francisco on June 17th 1842*. The artist, Arthur Stoessel, was one of the officers that took part in the voyage. Leaving New York in 1838 with the task of exploring Antarctica, Wilkes discovered the territories which he was to give his name to (but which Dumont d'Urville had already partially christened "Terre Adélie"), sailed back up to Borneo, visited the Sandwich Islands and returned along the coasts of Oregon and California. His discoveries were almost immediately questioned by the English Captain Ross, who claimed that there was nothing on the latitude and longitude he had indicated, and the existence of Wilkes Land was only confirmed quite recently, after the voyages of Sir Douglas Mawson between 1911 and 1914.

The second picture is called *Lost in the Weddel Sea* (Anonymous, American School, 19th Century) and recounts a dramatic episode during another American expedition, this time that of Benjamin Morrell. Between 1823 and 1839 Benjamin Morrell made four circumnavigations of the earth, the last of which was to finish tragically on the coast of Mozambique. The episode depicted in the painting (discovered in Morrell's sea-chest after his death, though he is certainly not the artist) is related in Volume VII of his journal: while returning from his second voyage, which had taken him successively to New Guinea, New Caledonia, New Zealand, Tasmania, the Kerguelen and Crozet Islands and the Prince Edward Islands, his ship became lost in the icy fogs of the Weddell Sea where, threatened by pack-ice, it wandered for several weeks. The canvas shows this tiny craft, confronted with enormous icebergs, and its whitish-gray tones would possess an almost Turneresque violence, if the naivety of the line did not destroy the effect.

The third picture's title is: *The Death of Juan Diaz at the Hands of Indians*, and it was painted by Arnold Hosenträger. After discovering Yucatan with Pinzon, Juan Diaz de Solis tried to press on into the bay of Rio de Janeiro, but fell into the hands of cannibal Indians who devoured him along with his companions. This painting, the fussy historicism of which barely conceals its self-complacent formalism, shows a group of half-naked Indians gathered in a clearing, which is bordered with the most luxuriant vegetation imaginable. In the middle, a large cauldron has been hung from three tree-trunks, forming a tripod; around it, the unfortunate Europeans have been tied to stakes, with the sole exception of a priest in a soutane who, on the extreme right of the picture, is kneeling, his hands together, while being hacked to death by two savages with axes. The work won the Silver Medal at the Louisville Salon of 1888.

The other two works of American origin are by Heinrich Kürz himself and are those which he decided to include in the *Gallery Portrait* as traces of his past and future work.

The first, *The Yacht Basin at Amagansett*, depicts a long white beach under an almost transparent sky. The sea is grey, dotted with yachts with pointed sails. A group of people, all clad in black, walk along the beach towards a large pink-and-green striped parasol under which an old woman sells slices of water melon. Kürz first met the Raffke family while he was painting this picture (they are the figures in black on the beach) and Hermann Raffke liked it so much that he bought it at once for two hundred dollars.

The second work does not exist, or rather it exists only as a small rectangle, two centimetres long by one centimetre across, in which, with the aid of a powerful magnifying glass, about thirty men and women can be made out throwing themselves off a landing-stage into the dark waters of a lake while, on the banks, crowds of people carrying torches run around in all directions. Heinrich Kürz once confided in Nowak that the only reason he had learnt how to paint was to be able, one day, to produce this picture and if he had not abandoned his art it would have been called *The Bewitched of Lake Ontario* and have been inspired by an event that occurred in Rochester in 1891 (Gustave Reid turned the story into a fairly successful novel in 1907): during the night of November 13/14th, a group of fanatical iconoclasts, which had been set up six months earlier by an employee of the Western Union, a beef butcher and a maritime insurance agent, set about systematically pillaging Eastman Kodak's factories, storehouses and shops. Almost four thousand cases, five thousand photographic plates and eighty-five kilometres of nitrocellulose film had been destroyed before the authorities could intervene. Pursued by half the town, the sect members threw themselves into the lake rather than give themselves up. Heinrich Kürz's father was among the seventy-eight victims.

The second Raffke Sale took place in Philadelphia from May 12th to 15th 1924, at Parke and Bernett's before a large crowd, which featured the East Coast's most famous collectors, accompanied by their advisors, and most of the directors of America's principal museums. The auctioneers were Messrs Moulineaux and Jonathan Cheap, both of whom had come specially from New York, expertly assisted by Messrs Rumkoff, Baldovinetti, Feuerabends and Turnpike Jr. The catalogue's three hundred and fifty-eight notices had been written by Messrs William Fleish and Humbert Raffke, with the help of the abovementioned experts and of Messrs Maxwell Parrish, Frantz Ingehalt, Thomas Greenback and Lester Nowak.

The first day was devoted to American painting and the first picture under the hammer was Adolphus Kleidrost's *Portrait of Bronco McGinnis*, the most tattooed man in the world; it was sold to Barnum's American Museum for

$2,500, which was one of the biggest bids of the session, along with John Jasper's *Small Florida Landscape* ($2,500), Adam Bilston's *Portrait of Mark Twain* ($2,000) and Mary Cassatt's *Old Coachman* ($5,000). Four other lots went for over five hundred dollars: Jefferson Abott's *Trapeze-Artist* ($825); Walter Ripley's vast composition *Immigrants*, depicting a motley crowd laden down with bundles, lined up on the deck of a large ship ($750); Frank La Scala's *The Fall of the House of Usher* ($650); and Walker Goosetail's *Taft and Colonel Waller's Marines Landing on Cuba in 1906*, which fetched only $600, despite the fact that his *Squaw* had been one of the first sale's successes. *The Yacht Basin at Amagansett* found a buyer at $125, Charles Wilkes made $98; *Two Small Cats Asleep*, *Whisky Drinkers* and *Café Waiters* were sold as one lot for $10; while *Tiger Hunting* climbed as high as $45.

The second day was given over to modern European painting and began with the auctioning of some twenty works classified as belonging to the "Neo-Classical School"; these included most of Hermann Raffke's *Lieblingssünde*. Over two-thirds of them went for less than fifty dollars, clear proof of how far this sort of painting had fallen out of favour since the beginning of the century. Seven of them, however, were the object of much livelier bidding and fetched far more than the experts' estimates: Rorret's *Field of the Cloth of Gold* ($450); Ferdinand Roybet's *Portrait of Mr Baudoin-Duhreuil as a Musketeer* ($1,200); Camille Velin-Ravel's *Launcelot* ($1,300); Gervex's *Insect Collector* ($1,750); Gérôme's *An Apothecary of Tunis* ($2,000); Jean Gigoux's *Portrait of a General* ($2,250); and Eugène Riou's extraordinary *Journey to the Centre of the Earth*, one of the few paintings by this artist who is more reputed as an engraver and illustrator ($2,500).

The afternoon session began altogether gloomily when three works were put up which Raffke had purchased on Albert Arnkle's advice: the *Self-Portrait with Masks*, by Ensor, whose reputation had not yet spread outside of Belgium, fetched only $250; while *Three Men on a Country Lane*, by August Macke, still almost unknown even in his native country although he had been dead for almost ten years, (Raffke bought this painting from him in 1908 while Macke was working in Berlin in Lovis Corinth's studio) made $83 from a starting price of $75; as for Gustav Klimt's *Portrait of an Austrian Officer*, it had difficulty reaching $560. But the atmosphere became decidedly more animated on the arrival of paintings from the French schools, whose international reputation had already been more or less established. Almost all of the lots went for more than a thousand dollars (Utrillo: *Flea-Market at Place Blanche*, $1,400; Vuillard: *Bourgeois Interior*, $2,000; Bonnard: *La Rue de l'Aveyron*, $2,800) and five of them for over ten thousand: Delacroix got $11,000 for his *Arabian Knights*, a fiery but rather loosely painted work; Renoir went up to $13,500 with his *Cigarette Sales-girl*; Cézanne to $17,000 with *Dominoes*, a robust still-life depicting a gaming table with a bouquet of pretty-by-night and a game of dominoes set out for play; as for Corot and Degas, they smashed through the experts' estimates, Corot with an Italian landscape in his early manner (a *View of Pompeii*) which reached $55,000, and Degas with his *Dancers* which peaked at $87,000.

The one-hundred-thousand dollar mark was reached the following morning when works from the German schools came under the hammer, and would be reached again on several occasions during the afternoon session and the next day, when paintings from the French, Flemish, Dutch and

Italian schools were put up in an increasingly electric atmosphere.

During these last two days, only six of the forty-five paintings that came up went for less than two thousand dollars. And the prices fetched by the other thirty-nine were often absolute records for the period:

$2,100: Flemish School (sometimes attributed to Marinus van Reymerswaele): *A Money-Changer and his Wife* (a period copy of Quentin Massys's famous picture; its chief interest lies in all the slight modifications that the copyist has made: thus, in the foreground, nobody's reflection appears in the little looking-glass; the old man (or woman) who can be seen in conversation through the half-open door in the background does not have a raised finger and the man listening does not have a hat; the miniature in the book which the banker's wife is looking at does not depict a Madonna with child, but a burial; and so on).

$3,800: German School, 16th Century (Hamburg): *Pyramus and Thisbe* (the imaginary Babylon which takes up the entire background of the canvas has often been cited as an example of that Hamburg mannerism which has left so regrettably few works).

$4,300: Flemish School: *The Fall of the Rebel Angels* (Cavastivali's suggested attribution of it to Bosch lacks any serious element of proof).

$5,000: Pietro Longhi: *Party at the Quarli Palace* (purchased by Mr William Randolph Hearst).

$6,500: French School: *Monk in Prayer* (sometimes

considered to be a *St Jerome*, despite the absence of a lion. This painting's history, as far as Nowak had been able to retrace it, is known only from 1793 when it was seized from Saint Saturnin's Church, Champigny, under the decrees concerning clerical property. From one auction to another it has successively been attributed to Valentin, to Honthorst, to Ter Brugghen, to Guido Reni, to Manfredi, to a "pupil of Caravaggio", to Schalken and to Lo Spagnoletto).

$7,500: Giovanni Paolo Pannini: *Architects* (two architects show a cardinal round the palace he is having built).

$8,000: Louis Boilly: *Alley with Musicians* (watched by a handful of idlers, a flautist, a violist and a cellist prepare to give a concert down a narrow side-street). A similar version, entitled *The Game of Quoits* (because, in the background of the scene, three children are playing a version of quoits, or "toad in the hole") is in the Saint-Germain Museum. This one came from Mlle Ursule Boulou's collection.

$11,000: Giovanni Battista Tiepolo: *The Birth of Venus* (ex Daddi Collection).

$11,540: Dutch School: *Chess Players* (there have been frequent attempts at attributing this painting to Karel van Mander. Nowak was able to show in a highly original way that this was impossible: for Mander died in 1606 and the pieces on the chessboard are set in the position following the fifteenth white move of the famous match played in 1625 by Giochino Greco, "The Calabrian". It should be noted that, in his copy of the painting, Kürz depicts the position after the eighteenth move, that is to say after the smothered mate).

$12,500: Arrigo Mattei: *Sleeping Musicians* (purchased by the Carnegie Foundation).

$13,125: Dutch School: *Young Girl Reading a Letter* (after long deliberations, the experts rejected its attribution to Metsu, or even to his workshop).

$13,200: Gerard van Honthorst ("Gherardo of the Night"): *Conflagration of Sodom* (belonged to the collections of Peter the Great. Elizavieta Petrovna gave it to Michel Lépicié in gratitude for his decoration of the Anichkov Palace in St Petersburg).

$14,000: Gerbrand van den Eeckhout: *Enée Fuyant les Ruines de Troie.*

$14,315: Joseph Vernet: *The Tempest* (this painting, quite close to the one in the Louvre, is known to have belonged to the collection of Viscount de Timbert, whose portrait by Baron Gros is still famous; but until then it had been known only from an engraving by Balechou).

$15,000: Peter von Cornelius: *Portrait of Wilhelm von Humholdt.*

$17,200: Sir Thomas Lawrence: *Portrait of Nelson* (of the four portraits of Nelson which this painter has left us, this one is indisputably the most romantic, for it does not show him holding his usual spy-glass in his remaining hand, but a medallion depicting Lady Hamilton).

$17,500: Peter Snayers: *The Siege of Tyre* (it was when he found a reproduction of this painting in one of Gilles van

Tilborg's *Gallery Portraits* that Nowak was able to identify the artist).

$17,900: Otto Reder: *The Sack of Troy* (purchased by the Sherburn-Boggs Foundation on behalf of the Smithsonian Athenæum of Schenectady, New York).

$18,250: Francois Gerard: *Cupid and Psyche* (the 1796 version, quite different from the 1798 version conserved in the Louvre).

$20,000: Leandro Bassano: *Portrait of an Ambassador* (purchased by the Corcoran Institute, Providence, Rhode Island).

$21,000: Jean-Baptiste Perronneau: *Portrait of his Reverence* (identified as François de Telek, Bishop of Klausenburg, whom the painter met during his travels in Russia in 1781).

$22,000 Gaspard Ten Broek: *A Picardy Landscape* (an extremely high price for this rather obscure painter who is often confused with Gerard Terborch or with Gaspard van der Brouckx).

$22,000: Jan Fyt: *Peacock and Fruit Basket* (Forcheville Collections, then Settembrini).

$25,000: School of Pisanello (?): *Portrait of a Princess of the House of Este* (Tauzia's opinion, rejecting an attribution to Pisanello, was confirmed by Rumkoff and Baldovinetti; Maxwell Parrish thought that the work might be by Pietro de Castelaccia, "Il Grossetto", but the lukewarm reception this hypothesis got from the other experts meant that it could not be accepted).

$32,000: Nicolas Poussin: *Manlius Capitolinus* (one of the six "subjects taken from Roman history" recorded by John Smith in his *catalogue raisonné* of 1837. Known from engravings by Massard and Landon, this work had been thought lost since 1870. Ingehalt rediscovered it in Berlin in 1891, in the coach-house of a hirer-out of carriages).

$37,500: Girodet-Trioson: *The Loing at Montargis* (Stendhal, who saw this painting at his friend Paul Bremont's house in Lyons in May, 1837, left a description of it in his *Memoires d'un Touriste*).

$38,000: Jean-Baptiste Greuze: *Orpheus and Eurydice* (Greuze painted few mythological scenes and they are generally not his best work; this one, a fine exception to the rule, dates to the same period as his *Danæ*, presented at the 1863 Salon, and so severely criticized).

$40,000: François Boucher: *The Riddle* (this picture, said to have been painted at the request of Catherine II, depicts three young girls, dressed in Moscovite fashion, who form a circle around a young man. Its title, given by the artist himself, has never been satisfactorily explained. In the *Gallery Portrait*, Kürz has dealt with this "riddle" in a particularly strange way. The first copy is an exact reproduction of the original, the sole exception being that the young man has become a skeleton armed with a scythe. In the second copy, the same scene now has seven children instead of three, these being Hermann Raffke's seven grandchildren. As for the third copy, it depicts another painting by Boucher, *La*

Fête Champêtre, a pastoral scene in which seventeen dancers and musicians move around a rocky forest interior: a woman plays a harp beside a fountain, the basin of which is an enormous sea-shell, reminiscent of a giant clam, with a spout in the form of a lion's head; three women dance together, forming the broad arc of a circle and, among them, two girls hold each other by the waist; a man plays a fiddle; and a girl in a grotto listens to a guitarist who sits at her feet. This is one of the few pictures that Hermann Raffke was unable to buy: announced at the Meyrat-Jasse Sale, it was sold by mutual agreement between the heirs and the Marquis of Pibolin, and withdrawn from the auction).

$50,000: Peter Paul Rubens: *Midas and Apollo* (from the former Antoine Cornelissen Collection, the man Van Dyck used to call Pictoriæ Artis Amator Antverpiæ). (Purchased by the Johnson Foundation, Connecticut.)

$62,500: Andrea Solario: *The Visitation* (purchased by Mr Simon Rawram of New York).

$65,000: Jean-Baptiste Siméon Chardin: *Luncheon Preparations* (purchased by the Sears Roebuck Foundation, Albany).

$85,000: Jan Steen: *Doctors* (less well-known than his *Doctor's Visit* in the Hague Museum, this work, which comes from the former collections of the Princess Palatine, and of which reworkings can be seen in the museums of Aarhus, Salamanca and Prague, contains a point of particular documentary interest: for, one of the doctors examines the young patient by putting to her half-unveiled breast a sort of ear-trumpet, quite similar to the "stethoscope" which

Laennec "invented" nearly one and a half centuries later; this no doubt explains why this work, valued by the experts at $40,000, was bumped up to double that price by the buyers for the Museum of Medical History at the University of Dartmouth).

$106,000: Carel Fabritius: *Young Girl with Harbour Chart* (purchased by the Museum of Hoaxville, Illinois).

$112,000: Antonio Pisano, called Pisanello: *The Annunciation* (purchased by the Associated Museums of Florida).

$120,000: Hans Holbein the Younger: *Portrait of the Merchant Martin Baumgarten* (purchased by the Budweiser Institute of Pittsburgh).

$137,000: Lucas Cranach the Elder: *Portrait of Jakob Ziegler* (purchased by the Vanderbilt Institute for the Development of Fine Arts, Troy).

$143,000: Giorgione: *Venus Giving the Arms of Vulcan to Aeneas* (the presentation of this picture under this title raised a few murmurs of disapproval in the sales room and one person got to his feet to demand that the work be presented as "attributed to Giorgione by Professor Nowak"; this did not stop its being the object of extremely tight bidding between the Metropolitan Museum, the Leichenhalle Foundation and the Art Institute of Chicago, which finally won the day).

$165,000: Frans Hals: *Portrait of Juste van Ostrack and of his Six Children* (from the former Duke of Marlborough Collection. Purchased by Treven Stewart, the art dealer, on behalf of a New York collector, the only thing known about him being that he was a family descendant).

$181,275: Jan Vermeer of Delft: *The Stolen Epistle* (purchased by the Edgar A. Perry Foundation of Baltimore).

A few years later, the directors of those public and private institutions which had acquired paintings as the second Raffke Sale received a letter, signed by Humbert Raffke, informing them that most of the works they had bought were fakes, and that he had painted them.

In 1887, while his uncle was in Europe, Humbert, then a student at the School of Fine Arts in Boston, had shown the collection to one of his teachers who, after a swift examination of the paintings which the brewer had amassed during his first three trips, had told him that they were either fakes or worthless.

On his return, Hermann Raffke was immediately informed, and decided to get his revenge. With the help of his children, of his nephew who, it turned out, was a brilliantly talented pasticheur, and of a few supernumeraries and accomplices, including Lester Nowak and Frantz Ingehalt, he set up an operation which would, many years later – and even after his death – allow him to mystify in his turn the art collectors, experts and dealers. His last eight trips to Europe were almost entirely given over to assembling or forging proofs of authenticity for the works which Humbert Raffke, alias Heinrich Kürz, was meanwhile producing. The keystone to this patient plot, every step of which had been carefully planned, was the creation of the *Gallery Portrait* in which, by depicting the paintings in his collection as copies, pastiches and reworkings, they would quite naturally look like copies, pastiches and reworkings of *genuine* paintings. The rest was a matter of the counterfeiter's art, that is to say of old panels, old canvases, workshop productions, craftily touched-up minor works, of pigment, glaze and *craquelure*.

The careful inspections that were carried out soon showed that most of the paintings from the Raffke Collection were indeed fakes, as fake as most of the details in this fictional tale, invented solely for the pleasure – and the thrill – of deception.

*TRANSLATOR'S
ACKNOWLEDGMENTS*

I should like to acknowledge the help and encouragement I have received from various members of the Association Georges Perec and especially David Bellos, Ela Bienenfeld, Hans Hartje and Patrizia Molteni. All mistakes, of course, remain my own.   I. M.

A NOTE ON THE TYPE

THREE BY PEREC has been set in Minion, a type designed by Robert Slimbach in 1990. An offshoot of the designer's researches during the development of Adobe Garamond, Minion hybridized the characteristics of numerous Renaissance sources into a single calligraphic hand. Unlike many faces developed exclusively for digital typesetting, drawings for Minion were transferred to the computer early in the design phase, preserving much of the freshness of the original concept. Conceived with an eye toward overall harmony, its capitals, lower case, and numerals were carefully balanced to maintain a well-groomed "family" resemblance – both between roman and italic and across the full range of weights. A decidedly contemporary face, Minion makes free use of the qualities the designer found most appealing in the types of the fifteenth and sixteenth centuries. Crisp drawing and a narrow set width make Minion an economical and easy going book type, and even its name reinforces its adaptable, affable, and almost self-effacing nature, referring as it does to a small size of type, a faithful or favored servant, and a kind of peach.

Design and composition by Carl W. Scarbrough

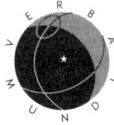

VERBA MUNDI BOOKS

VERBA MUNDI *offers the best in modern world literature –
whether by such established masters as José Donoso and Isaac
Babel, or by some of the world's most notable young writers,
many of them making their first appearance here in English.
By offering these superbly translated, attractively designed vol-
umes – now in a uniform paperback format – we mean to invite
adventurous readers to partake in a diversity of cultures.*

A Love Made Out of Nothing
& Zohara's Journey
by Barbara Honigmann

TRANSLATED FROM THE GERMAN BY JOHN S. BARRETT

WINNER OF THE KORET JEWISH BOOK AWARD FOR 2003
In these two brilliant, complementary novellas, two very different women struggle to rise from the ashes of their former selves. The narrator of *A Love Made Out of Nothing* leaves Berlin to start a new life as a student in Paris. Although she has escaped from her stifling past, she finds herself isolated, frightened, and still tied to her old existence by her complex relationship with a possessive and manipulative father. *Zohara's Journey* tells the story of a devoutly religious Sephardic Jew repatriated to southern France during the Algerian War. Married to a duplicitous rabbi, she lives alone in Strasbourg now that he has abandoned her. In her desperate efforts to locate him, Zohara comes to question both the man she thought she knew and the religion that has shaped them both. With these two intimate novellas, Godine is proud to introduce to North America a powerful new voice from Germany, one that speaks directly to the nature of isolation and, ultimately, to the necessity of self-reliance.

176 PAGES SOFTCOVER $16.95

Human Parts
by Orly Castel-Bloom

TRANSLATED FROM THE HEBREW BY DALYA BILU

In much the way Robert Altman gave us Nashville, Orly Castel-Bloom gives us contemporary Tel Aviv, a city long plagued with terrorist ambushes and suicide bombings. And now, suddenly, the city is further plagued – by a "Saudi flu" that is overcrowding the hospitals, by a failing economy, and by hailstones as big as soccer balls. And yet, against this background of monumental affliction and institutionalized emergency, the entire population, from kibbutz to Knesset, is trying to get on with its daily life – an endeavor at once tragic and comic, heroic and banal, real and surreal. From the Israeli president to a single mother of three, from an impoverished dry cleaner to a optimistic beauty-school student, Orly Castel-Bloom gives us a cross-section of interrelated persons struggling to bring calm, continuity, and normalcy to their extraordinarily restless lives. The result is a sardonic, topical, and wholly engrossing tour de force by one of Israel's best young novelists.

256 PAGES HARDCOVER $24.95

In the Flesh
by Christa Wolf

TRANSLATED FROM THE GERMAN BY JOHN S. BARRETT

Suffering severe abdominal pain, a woman is rushed to the emergency room. Her condition, her soaring temperature, her deepening distress – her symptoms all confound her doctors, who operate repeatedly. Drifting in and out of consciousness, she journeys through limbo, through the past, through her own memory, trying to understand the ethereal figures, signs, and portents of her twilight existence. The scene, half-real, half-hallucinated, is East Germany, a country of secrets, silences, and unexplained disappearances. The time: just before the fall of the Berlin Wall.

Christa Wolf's mesmerizing short novel, with its layers of meaning and elliptical content, is a supreme work of political and philosophical insight by one of Germany's greatest living writers. Alive with metaphor and myth, rich in symbolism and literary reference, still cooled by the chilly recollection of a monstrous regime, it draws a nuanced, witty, utterly compelling portrait of a person and a society close to death, yet still capable of recovery.

224 PAGES HARDCOVER $24.95

Last Trolley from Beethovenstraat
by Grete Weil

TRANSLATED FROM THE GERMAN BY JOHN S. BARRETT

From the author of *The Bride Price* comes a dark and haunting story of memory, guilt, and the meaning of responsibility.

Andreas, a once-promising poet, lives with his bride, Susanne, in postwar Germany. But although surrounded by the trappings of comfort and success, Andreas is obsessed by the memory of Susanne's younger brother, Daniel, whom he had sheltered in Amsterdam, but who was eventually deported by the Gestapo. The war over, Andreas rebuilds his life in the "new" Germany, trying to recapture Daniel through marriage to his sister. But he is unable to write or to find peace, unable to forget his torture over Daniel or the harrowing days and nights of th Occupation. Finally, he returns to Amsterdam to confront his memories of the war – for it was there that Andreas first recognized the horror inflicted by his own people, as every night he witnessed the round-up of the city's Jews beneath his window. And it was there that he came to the realizations about himself, his past and his heritage that give the story its resonance.

272 PAGES HARDCOVER $23.95

3 by Perec
by Georges Perec
TRANSLATED FROM THE FRENCH BY IAN MONK

INTRODUCTIONS BY DAVID BELLOS

George Perec, author of the acclaimed *Life A User's Manual*, is one of the great pleasure-givers of modern literature. Here, in one career-spanning volume, are three "easy pieces" from this smiling *maestro* of the typewriter keyboard. Published in 1966, "Which Moped with Chrome-Plated Handlebars at the Back of the Yard?" is a comic meditation on a serious subject: the moral imperatives of war – and of war-resistance. It tells the story of the hopelessly convoluted attempt by a group of Parisian intellectuals to save one of their fellows from being drafted into the French-Algerian conflict. "The Exeter Text" (1972) is the B-side to Perec's astounding tour-de-force *A Void* (1969), the novel in which he successfully avoided using the letter *e*. Here Perec pens the perfect reverse: he bleeds fevered, demented, clever sentences that set free the letter e's secret essence: sex. "A Gallery Portrait" (1979) was the last work Perec completed before his untimely death at the age of forty-six. It is the story of a painting – or, more precisely, of a painter and his patron – and a final exploration of many of Perec's signature themes: authenticity, forgery, valuation, mimesis, and purity of imagination.

192 PAGES SOFTCOVER $18.95

"53 Days"
by Georges Perec
EDITED BY HARRY MATHEWS AND JACQUES ROUBAUD

TRANSLATED FROM THE FRENCH BY DAVID BELLOS

Perec was working on this literary thriller at the time of his death in 1982. He left eleven completed chapters and extensive notes, and from these his friends Mathews and Roubaud assembled the outlines of the unfinished mystery while providing the reader with a fascinating window into the author's mind as he constructed his literary conundrum. As Mathews comments, "If death had not prevented Perec from completing this book, we would today be reading a masterpiece, one in the mold of Nabokov's *Pale Fire.*" But this is as close as it will get and, even unfinished, it is well worth the consideration.

272 PAGES HARDCOVER $23.95

W, or The Memory of Childhood
by Georges Perec
TRANSLATED FROM THE RENCH BY DAVID BELLOS
From the author of *Life A User's Manual* comes an equally astonishing novel – two parallel novels, to be precise, each aesthetically complete yet casting a distant light on the other. "One of these texts," explains the author, "is entirely imaginary: a reconstruction of a childhood fantasy about an land in thrall to the Olympic ideal. The other is an autobiography: a fragmentary tale of a wartime boyhood." Each text explores the innocence of childhood, the cruelty of the childish imagination, and the child's simplistic conception of justice – the black-and-white absolutism of winning and losing, of life and death. Together, the two stories form a fictional meditation on the Holocaust, that deserves a place on the same shelf as Günter Grass's *Tin Drum*.

176 PAGES SOFTCOVER $16.95

Things: A Story of the Sixties & A Man Asleep
by Georges Perec
TRANSLATED FROM THE FRENCH BY

DAVID BELLOS & ANDREW LEAK
In these two novels, the great French novelist ponders both sides of the materialistic impulse – that is, the desire to acquire a mass of shiny new things that will give life a semblance of stability and meaning. In *Things* a young middle-class couple "wants life's enjoyment, but all around them enjoyment is equated with ownership." They are paralyzed with covetousness, caught between "the film they would have liked to live in" and the disappointment of their unglamorous daily lives. In *A Man Asleep*, a young student is paralyzed by exactly the opposite – the desire to shed all possessions "and to want nothing, just to wait, until there is nothing left to wait for." Between these extremes of acquisitiveness and asceticism lies a third way, and Perec points toward it with detachment, compassion, and a very rare sense of humor.

224 PAGES SOFTCOVER $16.95

Days of Anger
by Sylvie Germain
TRANSLATED FROM THE FRENCH BY CHRISTINE DONOUGHER

Deep in the forests of Moran, far from civilization, live families of wood-cutters and shepherds. A remote and beautiful world, it is a place where madness still reigns, murder occurs, and bloody punishments are delivered. What has happened to the body of the sensual and beautiful Catherine Corvol, wife of a rich landowner, killed not out of hatred but an excess of love? Around this central enigma, Germain has created a gothic enchantment, a dazzling rural fantasy rich in angels, obsession, and revenge where the reader is carried forward as much by the lyricism of her prose as by the macabre and fantastic turns of the plot.

192 PAGES   SOFTCOVER $18.95

The Book of Nights
by Sylvie Germain
TRANSLATED FROM THE FRENCH BY CHRISTINE DONOUGHER

Winner of six literary prizes, this novel combines the timeless power of medieval legend, the resonance of Greek tragedy, and the harsh immediacy of a newsreel. Germain traces a century in the life of the Peniel family, from the Franco-Prussian War to World War II – a tale of triumph and loss, eroticism and holocaust, and the endless cycle of birth and death. *"Original and compelling.... Takes [magic and realism] to the outer limit and then fearlessly hurls one against the other."* – New York Times Book Review *(Notable Book of the Year, 1993)*

272 PAGES   HARDCOVER $22.95

Night of Amber
by Sylvie Germain
TRANSLATED FROM THE FRENCH BY CHRISTINE DONOUGHER

In the sequel to her acclaimed *The Book of Nights*, Germain continues the grotesque, fantastic, and riveting story of the tragic Peniel family in a whirlwind novel that skillfully blends European history, myth, invention, and fantasy, tracing their fortuned from the end of World War II through the Algerian War to the frenzied Paris of 1968.

272 PAGES   HARDCOVER $23.95